VINDICATION

Copyright © New Author Publishing

ISBN: 9781068642012

Vindication

*

Elizabeth Muir Lewis

CHAPTER ONE

Jamie stood in the town square, kicking his heels. His cousin Alix slouched against the railings.

He was a local lad. He and Jamie had known each other all their lives, as their mothers were sisters. Every year, Jamie came to the town while his parents were away; they were actors, and every summer they went on tour.

"Och, how can you live in such a godforsaken place?" Jamie grumbled.

"It's not so bad. Better than noisy Edinburgh; I couldn't stand that."

Jamie sighed. How could Alix say that? He personally loved the city: the crowds; the noise; always something to do. Not like here: a small, provincial town with one decent café and a fleapit cinema.

Cigarettes dangling self-consciously on their lips made them feel grown up as they lounged against the gateposts, hands in pockets, watching people as they passed.

"What's on at the fleapit?"

"Just an old Laurel and Hardy."

"I saw that in Edinburgh – bloody funny, actually. Let's go; I could easy see it again."

"Okay. How about fish and chips before the matinee?"

"Righty-ho."

The bells from the church pealed out, filling the square with mind-numbing clamour.

Not for the first time, Jamie wondered why he came here every summer; it was always such a drag. He stayed with an aunt – another sister! Why couldn't he have parents who were there all the time, instead of the rather mad, disorganized couple who had left to tour the country, leaving their offspring to lodge with whomever would have him?

Madly artistic, they were totally unable to understand this son of theirs. To these thespians, anyone who found mathematics thrilling, as Jamie did, was as alien as a Martian.

"I've no idea where he came from, John," his mother would say. "Must be a throwback."

"Yes, dear. I believe there was someone odd, long ago."

This year, Jamie had, as usual, gone to a small village near Montrose, where an aged aunt and uncle lived. The uncle was a past headmaster who believed in the old ways.

"Discipline, dear boy," he would say at every breakfast, "all been lost, everyone doing what they want. Nothing like a few whacks occasionally."

Aunt Polly was an ex-matron. Old school. She would measure Jamie's bath level, which he hated. "I'm not a kid still, Auntie," he would complain.

In a funny way, he was fond of them. Their house was a typical Scottish one: grim, grey stone with nothing to relieve the dour, cold exterior. Inside, it had furniture which came from an era when good, solid mahogany was the fashion: huge wardrobes and a grandfather clock, which chimed every quarter with ponderous clarity. The dining room housed an enormous table, with a centrepiece of some battle, done in porcelain; at meals, Jamie would be on the side where grotesque faces leered out at him, grinning and menacing. At least he could hide behind it, so his uncle couldn't see him.

Conversation was not encouraged at meals – his uncle didn't believe in small talk – so breakfast and dinner were eaten in broody silence. If Jamie only knew that the presence of a young man was an unsought penance for these old people. He disturbed their tranquil life. They had nothing to say and certainly didn't understand the world he lived in, positively disapproving of it most of the time.

"Your sister and brother-in-law are far too lax with Jamie."

"Well, they are artistic, dear."

This would elicit a grunt of disapproval; artistic was not among the attributes that Uncle approved of. The fact that Jamie intended to be a doctor made little difference.

"He's got to pass exams, you know. I doubt he has the application."

Every morning, Jamie went out. Although he had studies to do, by the end of breakfast he only wanted to get some fresh air, meet his cousin and idle the day away, before he had to get back. This morning, he decided to get away earlier.

"Now, mind you're in for tea, Jamie," his aunt said as he went out, "or there will be none for you. You know how Uncle hates lateness."

"I do, Auntie. See you later, then."

But that morning, as Jamie and Alix lounged in the square, something happened which changed things...

As the bells suddenly stopped, leaving their ears ringing, a girl passed. Both boys whistled.

"What a beauty," Alix said, loud enough for the girl to hear. She tossed her head, giving them a flirtatious glance.

Jamie watched her as she crossed the square: blonde hair down to her waist; a slim figure, in tight jeans which showed off her slender waist; long legs in high heels, tapping; and a swaying, seductive walk.

"Wow, some figure!"

"I'll say."

The girl disappeared around the corner by the church, giving one more look, their gaze idly following her as she disappeared.

Now they had all day to fill.

"Forget fish and chips; let's have beans on toast in the café, then go to the flick."

"Okay."

Wolfing down his beans, with a cup of tea, Jamie wondered why he had thought the girl who passed so lovely; she wasn't his type at all. *I suppose she was gorgeous.*

In the half-empty cinema, they sat in the front row eating popcorn, enjoying the antics of the American comedians and laughing at the advertisements.

By the time it was over, it was nearly dark.

"Blimey! I've missed tea at the prison!" Jamie joked.

Alix laughed. "Let's meet up tomorrow. Don't forget the match."

There was a football match being played between Montrose and Edinburgh the next day – local stuff, but popular with the community, where the youth of Montrose met to cheer their side on.

"See you then. 'Bye."

And now another tedious evening to look forward to – and he'd be in Uncle's bad books.

Getting back, he met a wall of silence, Uncle choosing to ignore him, austere glances saying it all.

Auntie, as usual, fluttered around, trying to make up for her husband. "Don't you worry, Jamie, he'll get over it. Pity you couldn't try to get back in time, dear."

"I'm really sorry, Auntie. Alix and I went to a film, and I didn't realize how long it would be."

"I do understand, you know. It's just that your uncle finds this modern world difficult. It's all so different to how it used to be."

In spite of himself, Jamie felt sorry for his aunt, seeing how difficult his uncle made her life. He was really very fond of her. She was one of those women who'd had a life of having to put up with a man who expected her to obey his every decree. With her sparse, brown hair and watery eyes, always seemingly on the edge of weeping, she was a fragile and indecisive person. Jamie wanted to take her in his arms, to try to comfort her, but he knew that would never do; she had built a protective barrier between her and the world.

Supper was at six on the dot, and always the same food; ham and scones, with sparse butter. Uncle didn't believe in waste or indulgence. He cut the bread every night, and every night gave Jamie a lesson in bread-cutting. Tonight was no exception. "A steady hand – that's the secret."

"Yes, Uncle." Didn't he remember that he'd said that before?

After it was over, Uncle said some prayers then Jamie went upstairs. He had studies. If his exams were good, he would qualify for medical school.

His parents had always assumed he would follow them. So, when he announced that he wanted to be a doctor, they were both astonished and dismayed.

"We had hoped you might follow us into the theatre, Jamie. You were always pretty good when you took parts in the school play. We had high hopes, dear."

How could he tell them that the life of an actor was the last thing he wanted? Touring, cheap digs, no family life and not much profit; his parents always seemed to be hard up. Jamie yearned for stability, a life with routine, knowing where he would be at any given time. He knew these two people would despise him for that. They loved what he hated.

He worked for a few hours before rolling into bed – to dream about a lovely, young girl with long hair down to her waist.

CHAPTER TWO

The next morning, after breakfast, he decided to go for a ride on his bike.

Uncle was not going to let him go without a fuss.

"Where are you going today, Jamie?" he asked. "I assume you will be careful who you spend time with? You should be upstairs, working."

"I will, Uncle, I promise. I just thought I would get some fresh air first."

"That's good, Jamie," his aunt said. "Just be careful, dear, you don't fall off your bike."

Two old people, their faces lined with care and worry, one with a denied maternal caring, the other a disapproval from habit.

I wish they wouldn't treat me like a child. They meant well, but it was jolly irritating.

He set off – no particular direction. It was a fresh, sunny morning, and dew still lay on the grass. Cycling along, he could smell the hay in the fields, the cut grass from mown lawns.

Up to now, the road had been on the flat but, turning into a lane, he saw he was at the top of a steep hill. This would be fun!

He set off, braking to stop himself going too fast, then freewheeling, gathering speed.

As he got to the foot of the hill, he saw a girl on a bike coming toward him.

By now he was going too fast to stop, and they sped toward each other.

The girl fell off, into the grass.

Jamie managed to stop and went back.

"Hey, I'm sorry! Are you alright?"

She was getting up, her back to him. "Aye, I'm fine." She looked up at him. She was the girl in the square. Long, blonde hair cascading down to her waist. Big, blue eyes. Jamie swallowed.

"I've seen you before. I say, are you really alright?"

"Yes, honestly. I must get home, though." She dusted down her skirt, gave him a smile and set off.

Jamie watched her until she disappeared. What a pillock he was; he hadn't even asked her name, standing there gawping like a klutz. Well, too late; she'd gone. Jamie went home.

Lunch was ready and Uncle gave him an interrogation: what had he been doing; where did he go? Jamie didn't tell him about the girl; that was a secret. Anyway, he could imagine what Uncle would say:

"Girls? You keep away from them, laddie. Never do you any good."

Auntie would then smile, and probably ask him questions after Uncle had gone for his afternoon nap.

He spent the afternoon studying, then went to meet Alix for the football match.

Hundreds of young men mashed together, singing, cheering and waving flags. Then, in the pub after, swigging beer and playing darts.

Somehow, during the match he had torn his trousers. When he got back, Auntie saw the tear.

"What you young people get up to I can't imagine," Auntie said.

"Now, let me mend that, dear. No need to take them off; just bend over."

Jamie leant on the sill of the window, as she set about the mend. He watched the people walking by. Then a girl passed.

It was her! The girl on the bike.

She saw him and waved. He waved back. How mortifying! Could she see Auntie sewing up his backside?

"Do you know that girl, Auntie?"

She peered over his shoulder. "Aye, that's the Macdonald girl. Lives down the street, in number ten. Jeannie, she's called."

Jeannie. A nice name. Suited her. Jeannie with the light-brown hair – except hers was golden. Soft, golden curls.

"There, Jamie, that should do." His aunt nipped off the thread. "Just don't move too fast," she smiled, giving him a kiss.

The rest of the afternoon was spent studying. Time was getting on, with only two weeks left to finish his set projects, but he was pretty well ahead.

After supper, he sauntered out.

Should he call on Jeannie? Knock on the door of number ten? Would her mother shout at him? Or, worse still, her father?

"Who are you?" they might ask.

"Well, I will be a doctor one day." Would that sound respectable enough?

He walked down the street: number eight... nine... ten; there it was.

Suddenly he got cold feet. His heart beat faster.

What on Earth am I nervous about?

Lifting the knocker, it dropped with a noise like thunder. Footsteps came and the door opened.

A very large woman stood there, arms folded.

"Aye, and what do you want? I'll have no political at my door."

"No," he gasped, "I'm no' political. I've come to see Jeannie."

She seemed to grow bigger. "There's no Jeannie here! Jean is her name! I'll no' have a good name mucked about with. Good day." With that, she slammed the door shut, leaving him feeling a bit of a fool. Neighbours were looking over, some smiling.

He stood there for a moment...

...Then heard: "Pst! Pst!"

There, at a window, stood his angel, a finger to her lips and a big, shy, blue-eyed smile.

"Help me down, you big lummock."

With his hands around her slender waist, he helped her down, the scent of rose water and newly washed hair hitting his nostrils. It was intoxicating having her so near. A tendril of hair tickled his face.

"You're beautiful."

"So why did you ignore me this morning?"

No way would he tell her that his auntie was sewing up his breeks, on his backside. "Will you walk with me?"

"Aye, of course." She took his arm.

Footsteps matching, they walked down the street.

Jamie felt grown up and, if he was honest, a bit nervous. He had known very few girls, and none as lovely as Jeannie. He wanted to get it right.

"Would you like to go to a film this evening, Jeannie?"

"That would be nice. I hear there's a Laurel and Hardy film on. I'd like to see that."

He wasn't going to tell her he'd already seen it twice!

"Come on, let's have something to eat in the café and catch the first showing."

In the cinema, they laughed and she snuggled up close. Her scent was intoxicating, her body warm and sweet. She had a way of throwing her head back when she laughed. He watched her more than he did the film. She was enchanting.

It was dark when they came out, the streets dimly lit under the streetlamps.

"I'll walk you home, Jeannie."

She took his arm but, plucking up courage, Jamie took her hand. She didn't pull away. Then he slipped an arm around her waist. He was doing well; she stayed close, in his embrace.

"Would you like to go somewhere nice, Jamie?" she asked.

"If you want."

Pulling him by his hand, she led him into an alleyway, which was pitch black. Then, suddenly, she was in his arms, kissing him.

"Oh, Jamie, that's good."

Yes, it was. But then Jamie was getting a little bit scared, as she pulled him farther through wrought iron gates, into what looked like a graveyard, the gravestones shining white under the moon.

"No one ever comes here. Come on, Jamie." She sank down onto the grass. "Here, come on; sit with me."

He sat down.

She took his hand and guided it underneath her short dress. She was naked!

"There, now, that's what you've been wanting, isn't it, Jamie?"

She took off her dress. Lying naked in the moonlight, she was unashamed, inviting him.

He groaned. He was a man, but he didn't want... this. Not like that.

"I'm sorry, Jeannie. I really can't."

"I'm prepared, if that's what's making you nervous."

Was this his angel? His innocent young girl? Who was doing the seducing here? He got up.

"I'll take you home, Jeannie. Put your dress back on."

He was not prepared for what happened next.

"Oh, indeed? You fine young man! Trying to take advantage of me, were you? Well, we'll soon see about that." With anger and humiliation, she put her dress back on and, without waiting, flounced away. Jamie watched as she ran up the alleyway. He could hear her crying.

He stayed sitting on the grass. Had he been a cad? Should he have done what she had so obviously been begging for? No, he didn't want it to be like that.

He slowly got up. He could hardly believe what had happened. What had started as sweet and pure had turned ugly and sordid. And this lovely girl had done it before – that was obvious.

He got up and walked back to his aunt and uncle's.

"Did you have a nice time, dear?" asked his aunt.

"Yes, fine, Auntie."

"If it's the Macdonald girl you were with, be careful, Jamie; she can be a wild child."

"I shan't be seeing her again. We had a nice evening, that's all."

His aunt smiled at him, though she could see her nephew was hurting. "You can tell me, dear. I won't pass it on."

"Thank you, Auntie, it's fine. I'll get to bed, and probably get up early to study."

For the next few days, he lived in fear of meeting Jeannie, but never saw her.

Then finally the time came to leave. His parents had returned from their tour.

"Goodbye, Auntie. Thanks for everything."

"It's been lovely having you, Jamie. Give our love to your mother and father."

On the train back to Edinburgh, Jamie turned over in his mind what had happened. He still couldn't believe it. He still felt that disappointment. He wondered if there was something wrong with him. Wouldn't most men have taken advantage? He knew he wasn't gay, so what was it?

Well, I'll never know.

Deep down, he knew he was glad he had been strong enough to say no.

Some puritanical throwback – that's what I am, he thought, grinning to himself.

CHAPTER THREE

His parents were already back when he got to the family apartment. It was a three-bedroomed, spacious place, rarely tidy; his parents didn't believe in worrying about such things. If any tidying and cleaning was done, it was Jamie's job.

"Darling!" his mother cried. "We missed you so much!"

She was a tall, rather showy woman, with a tendency to wear a kaleidoscope of colours which had little connection with each other. She specialized in roles which had tragic overtones, as she was rather good at expressing dramatic and dark moods.

His father was tall, too. In fact, they made a fine couple. He was dark, with a short beard. His forte was comedy; he could captivate an audience with his gift for the nuances of humour. With a raised eyebrow, he could insinuate. With his back turned to the audience, he could express a comedic situation.

"How was my sister, Jamie?" his mother enquired.

"She was okay, Ma… Uncle bosses her around."

"I know. He's an awful man. I never liked him."

It was nice to be home. Jamie unpacked, and that evening they had a meal together, in warm family rapport. Just for a while, Jamie had what he yearned for: a family, together.

It was only a week until he went back to school. He spent it doing his work. He was ready. He had to get pretty high grades to qualify for medical school, but he was confident.

*

The first day back, old friends greeted each other, boasting of conquests. Jamie kept quiet; Jeannie's name would not pass his lips. Anyway, it all now seemed like some bad dream.

But, the next day, the principal called him into the office.

"Jamie, has anything happened while you were on holiday?"

"No, sir."

"Well, I have some bad news, I'm afraid. I have heard, from a solicitor in Montrose, that a local girl is accusing you of rape."

Jamie stood there, stunned.

What?! Oh, my god!

"That's not possible, sir! Not true!"

"It's a serious accusation."

"I'm sorry, sir, but simply nothing happened."

"Well, Jamie, the problem with that is that if an accusation like this is made formal, it has to go ahead. If you are innocent, this is a terrible thing for you."

Jamie felt as if the world was crashing in on him. Suddenly he was accused of something he hadn't done. But how to prove it?

Had he made Jeannie so mad that she was out to get vengeance of some kind? In all innocence he had asked her out. How he wished he could take that back.

"What should I do, sir?" he asked the headteacher.

"Let me think about it. First things first: I would want to meet up with your mother and father. Could you arrange that? Also, I think you should go home for now. Let's try and keep it under wraps for as long as we can."

Jamie left the headteacher's room. Keep it under wraps, the head had said, but Jamie could just imagine what the other students would say. Then the press.

Oh, God, how has this happened?

He went home.

His parents were in the middle of learning lines for a new play.

"Hello, darling," called his mother. "Why are you home? Is school not starting?"

"Mum, Dad, can I have a talk with you?"

"Well, of course, darling. Let's have a coffee and then chat."

More than a chat! This was going to be hard. His parents were usually unaware of down-to-earth matters; they functioned on a plane of artistic unreality. They were going to get a shock.

"Here we are, darling." His mother brought in a tray of coffee mugs. "Now, what's this chat you want to have?"

"Have you been getting into trouble?" his father laughed. "Not in Montrose, surely?" He had given Jamie an opening.

"Well, actually, yes."

"Oh, darling, how wonderful! Interesting, I hope."

"Now, listen, both of you. Something has happened that I need help with – and, in Montrose, yes, Dad. Can I tell you the whole story?"

"Of course. We're listening."

Would they listen, or would they twist it around and not believe him? That would be the worst thing. Because, if they didn't believe him, who else would?

Taking a big breath, he told them – right from when he saw Jeannie in the square, helping her out of the window, taking her to the pictures, and then the bit in the graveyard.

"And that's the story. And she is accusing me of rape."

Neither parent spoke. Silence fell.

"Do you believe me?"

"Jamie," his father said, "we have lived with you since you were born, except for the occasional parting; I think I can safely say that I know you. And, if you say it never happened, then, yes, I believe you absolutely."

"Darling boy, you have got into the clutches of a bad girl, and quite obviously you hurt her pride when you refused to do what she was offering. But what to do now? John, what shall we do?"

"The first thing is to see a lawyer, and get some idea of what happens when you are accused of something like this. Let me think about it."

For the first time, Jamie saw that his two parents were aware of a situation. It was a comfort, for he felt, at the moment, like a sailor cast adrift. The calamity of what had happened was slowly sinking in. His life, all mapped out, was suddenly in danger. He'd read about similar cases: how a young life was ruined by slander and false claims. And the press: what hay they would make!

"Now, Jamie, let's not be hasty. First we must get advice."

That his parents were stunned there was no doubt. But they seemed to know that their son needed support, and they were surprising him.

For the next few days, they set about finding someone to advise them. John had some contacts, phoning a fellow actor who had been embroiled in a similar scandal.

"He has given me the name of a top defence lawyer, Jamie. I'm going to contact her – yes, it's a *she* – and set up a meeting."

"Won't this cost a lot?"

"Yes, Jamie, it will. I've given this some thought, though. I have a fund your mother and I set up some twenty years ago – it's worth a lot now, so I'm going to get it out and use it."

"Oh, Dad, that's terrible. Surely that was your retirement fund?"

"Darling," cried his mother, "you are our son, the most precious person in the world to us! We grudge not a penny."

It was strange. For the first time in his life, Jamie suddenly felt a closeness he had never had before for these two parents of his. When he needed them, they were there.

Over the next week, his father was making contacts and phone calls. Emails were flying back and forth. Until, one morning at breakfast, he cried: "We've got her! The best defence lawyer in the country!"

A meeting was set up with the lawyer, Jamie and his parents.

"Of course, we'll keep out of it, Jamie; we think the first meeting must be just you and her. I feel it is very important that she believes you."

Jamie had decided not to go to school. He didn't want to waste work time, and felt anger that what had happened might change his life. Also, it seemed that his fellow students had got wind of something: looks behind his back, whispers in corridors, sniggers as he passed... Even his best mates changed, avoiding him. He wanted to shout: "I thought you were friends!"

The meeting was arranged with the lawyer, Sally Maitland. Would a female lawyer be better than a male?

"I think a female will understand better," his mother suggested.

Jamie wasn't sure about that. After all, it was a female accuser. What if this Sally had sympathy for Jeannie?

Sally arrived on time. Jamie looked at her as she entered the room: well-dressed but not too fashionable; just enough to look successful. Dark hair wound into a chignon, glasses hiding some pretty intense eyes, and a businesslike, crisp speaker.

"Well, Jamie, this is a pretty awful thing happening to you."

"I guess you could say that."

"Okay, let's get onto a level of understanding, right from the word go. I defend you. I don't have to believe you; I just have to defend you. But I want and would prefer to believe you. So, what I want first is an absolutely true and detailed account of what happened that night."

"Yes, I can do that."

"Right. Start from the beginning, telling me everything."

Jamie began, telling Sally not only what happened or didn't happen, but his thoughts at the time, too.

"And so she left, crying with anger," he ended.

She thought for some time. "Well, that's quite a story. Now, what would a prosecutor ask you? Probably: why would a healthy, young man not take something offered to him by a beautiful young girl?"

"If I tell you why, you won't laugh?"

"I never laugh, Jamie. Go on, then."

"Well, it might seem pathetic, but what she was offering was something I thought should be with the girl I would marry. And it seemed so sordid. And a shock. I had thought her beautiful, adorable, and there she was, throwing her body at me."

Sally listened without interruption. She gazed at Jamie.

"You know, I believe you, which is important. What strikes me is how we can deal with this, so that your career and your future life are not affected."

"That worries me, too. I want to be a doctor."

"I know you do. So, what are the main problems? One is that it's her word against yours, and juries tend to believe the female in these cases. Remember those 'me, too' cases against Weinstein? Or, even worse, the ones against Domingo, the singer?"

"Is it that mud sticks even if there is none?"

"It can be. You are a bright boy. We are going to plan a strategy that might work. I have an idea. I will need some time to do some sleuth work."

After the talk was over, John and Linda brought a tray of tea in.

"I am confident that we can solve this, Mr. and Mrs. Lindsey."

"Do call us Linda and John."

"The most important thing is that, after Jamie told me the whole story, I believe him."

They chatted, then Helen left. Did he feel better? Jamie wasn't sure. It was a never-ending nightmare.

*

Things began to move. Letters came, asking that Jamie attend a pre-trial assessment. Then, what he had dreaded: the phone rang one morning…

"Is that Jamie Lindsey?"

"Yes."

"I understand that you are involved in a rape case."

"Who are you? None of your business."

"It's my job, matey; no need to get on your high horse. We get the news so we have to follow it. Is it true, then?"

"Are you a newspaper?"

"Aye, that's right: *The Edinburgh News*."

"Well, I can't help you."

"I'll find out anyway, let me tell you."

"Go ahead. Goodbye."

He felt sick. Was this what was going to happen? He still couldn't believe it. Just a week ago, he had his life mapped out. A terrible mistake was turning into a nightmare.

And worse was to come. His uncle phoned from Montrose.

"We have had a visit from the police, asking about Jamie; something about a rape accusation. We have never been so embarrassed. The neighbours are shunning us; the newspapers are ringing… What were you up to, Jamie, when you were staying with us?"

"Nothing, Uncle; it's all a mistake. It's that Macdonald girl down the street."

His aunt came on. "Oh, Jamie, dear! Remember, I warned you about her! This is a terrible thing."

They rang off, not even speaking to his parents.

What do I do? Jamie asked himself. He'd read about these sorts of case, but never did he think he would be embroiled in one – and one so frustratingly murky.

"Your word against hers," the lawyer had said, "and juries tend to believe the female."

I could go away, get lost. But that wouldn't solve anything. *I could shoot myself...* He grinned. That would make him look as though he was guilty. And he didn't fancy that, anyway.

Inside, he felt the dawning of something else. A determination. He was innocent, and he'd be damned if his life would be ruined by that lying little bitch!

Yes, that's what she is. Let's not pretend.

The weeks passed, until he had to go to the Edinburgh court for the first meeting.

What he hadn't expected was that Jeannie was there, too, with her parents. Her great big mother glared over at him, complicit and self-satisfied, scenting victory. Her father was a shrimp of a man, bald with a long, thin nose, terrified of his overbearing wife. Jeannie, dressed in a simple, very young-style dress, looked virginal and innocent. No longer the coquette, the seducer, here was the innocent victim.

It was mostly a formal meeting, nothing said about the case to be brought forward. A date was set for a trial.

Why a trial? Jamie thought. *Why not just talk about it, get Jeannie to admit she was lying?* But, no. Greed, that's what it was. If Jeannie, who knew she was lying, still maintained it, then what chance did he have?

The next few weeks were hell, the phone continually ringing. *BBC News* had got wind of it. *"SCOTS BOY ACCUSED OF RAPE"* the headlines announced. His name was even mentioned. Not Jeannie's; she was protected, which didn't seem fair to Jamie. This was a nightmare that was real.

In a funny sort of way, it all became so real that he forgot his other life. Would the press pick that up? After all, his parents were fairly well-known actors. Would this affect their work?

"How can we leave you, darling?" his mother cried, when he asked her.

The court case was in two weeks.

On the morning, as they left, his parents said: "Jamie, we are there for you, every step of the way."

"It's going to be fine, old chap," his father exclaimed.

"You can't know how that feels. Thanks, both of you. I'm just so sorry it's happened at all."

The court was full of people he knew when he got there.

"I wish they hadn't got wind of this, Jamie," said Helen. "But never mind. Let's see what we can do."

It didn't go well. Jamie was questioned and he answered the

prosecutor, but somehow it sounded a bit weak. When Jeannie was questioned, she gave the impression that here was a poor, wee little girl who had been ravished against her will. However hard the defence tried to break her down, she managed to find some tears, sobbing about how awful it had been; how Jamie was a monster, who had forced her against her will. Jamie could see no way that she would not be believed. He almost did so himself, she was so convincing.

"This girl is good," the lawyer said. "We have to find a way to get her to reveal herself."

"I don't see how. She's got the strong hand."

Jamie was out of his depth and he knew it. There was no defence against a girl who held all the cards.

Afterward, in the hall, she was standing with her family. She saw Jamie and, just for a second, her guard down, she gave him a look that seemed to say: *Sorry, I know you didn't do anything wrong.* But it was just for a second; her mother, seeing the look pass between them, smacked her daughter, pulling her away.

So, it's the mother, thought Jamie, *not Jeannie!* That, at least, was a comfort. It made it less hurtful, in a way. He told the lawyer.

"That's a good observation, Jamie. Maybe I should put Mum on the stand, see what I can come up with to break her down."

After the break, they went back inside. It was the defence who must now put their case; the result of this would take it to the higher court.

Sally took Jamie at his word and called on Jeannie's mother.

That this woman could have such a lovely daughter was a puzzle. She was a huge, big-busted woman with a coarse face and manner.

Sally asked her: "Mrs. Macdonald, can you assure me that your daughter is not in the habit of encouraging young men?"

"Och, I'll have you know that my wee girl is as pure as the driven snow. Why, she will hardly look at a young man without blushing. That one…" she pointed to Jamie "…took advantage of her! What he did was disgusting."

"If that is so, Mrs. Macdonald, can you explain why neighbours describe your daughter as a rather forward and flirtatious girl, who plays around with the affections of young men?"

Mrs. Macdonald seemed to swell as she stood. "I'll have you know that this is the nasty gossip of jealousy. That's all it is: jealousy."

Sally continued in this vein for some time, achieving what she set out to do: getting Mrs. Macdonald angry.

"And isn't this accusation just a pack of lies?"

Mrs. Macdonald almost frothed at the mouth.

Now it was the prosecutor's turn, as Jamie had to stand there and be examined. The prosecutor was an overweight, red-faced man. A drinker, by the look of him, with red nose and cheeks, his eyes bulbous and veined. Straggly hair was combed over to hide baldness.

"Tell me, Jamie," he began, "how is it that a fine young man refuses to enjoy what a beautiful young girl offers him? Do you expect us to believe that, in that graveyard, you didn't take what was available?"

"No, I didn't. I had not expected, when I walked Miss Macdonald out, that the night would end like that. I may sound unusual, but I did not want to do something that was against my long-held wish to wait, until I meet the girl I will marry."

It went on for a while like this. Jamie felt like he was in a nightmare: all those people watching, the press waiting, Jeannie sitting at a table in front of him. How did this happen? *Why are you doing this, Jeannie?* he just wanted to ask.

Soon it was over. The case would go to the higher court. Everyone went home.

"Darling Jamie," his mother said, as they drove home, "that girl is lying, and it's that dreadful mother who is pushing her! What are they hoping for? To make money out of this? To see you go to prison?"

"I don't know why, Ma. I just know it's agony, and wish it would stop."

The next court appearance was in a month. Jamie tried to work, but he didn't go to school; he was too much a figure of interest.

A career in medicine was now looking in doubt; how could he be a doctor if he had charges of rape hanging over him? He was almost feeling resigned.

Some relief came when his cousin Alix dropped in to see him. They went out into the town, to have a drink in a pub.

Edinburgh was quiet at that time of year. The festival was over and things were settling down, into the usual rhythm. The two boys walked down Princes Street, underneath the castle, finding a small place up a side street.

"Now, listen, Jamie. I've had an idea."

"Such as?"

"Well, from what I've read, no one is going to believe you while that girl maintains that you did what she claims, and plays the poor wee girl."

"That's what I'm afraid of."

"So, I've had a brainwave. Why don't I take up with Jeannie in some way? Meet her as if by accident and ask her out? Now, just suppose she does the same with me, and we end up in the graveyard, and I have a recording thing in my pocket?"

"You're mad, Alix. It won't work. She'll suspect something."

"Does she know we are cousins?"

"I doubt it."

"Well, isn't it worth a shot?"

"I suppose so. But it's risky. And would it be legal?"

"Maybe not. I could find out; I have a friend who is a lawyer. Anyway, even if it isn't legal, it could be a weapon. And, just in case you wonder what I'm thinking and do I believe you, I do. I saw that girl in the square, too, and if ever there was a flirt, she's it."

"Okay, Alix. You're a friend. Just don't do anything that gets you into trouble; one of us is enough."

"I'll give it some thought, and how best to set it up."

Jamie went off home, and Alix got a train back to Montrose.

When Jamie got back his parents were waiting for him, sitting on the sofa together, looking as though they had something to say.

"Jamie, darling, your father and I have been thinking. We are off to do a new play in Manchester, the day after tomorrow; we would like you to come with us."

"Mum, thanks, but what would I do?"

"Jamie," his father added, "first of all, it would be great to have you with us. Secondly, your mother will just worry herself sick all the time. And, thirdly, it could help take your mind off this whole business."

"And you could help us," his mother interrupted; "there would be jobs you could do. And we would be together."

Jamie listened. It was true that he had a month to wait until the case came to court again; he knew he would only fret. Besides, he had never been with his parents when they were acting; it could be interesting, and perhaps take his mind off of what was going on.

"Okay, Mum and Dad, you're on."

"Oh, darling, that's wonderful. Let's plan, and see how to do it all best. We have reserved a flat which has a third bedroom, so that's solved. Other than that, let's play it by ear."

Jamie was now committed. Whether he would find it a mistake or being with his parents would work out, he didn't know. So much had happened to him that he was beyond caring.

Next morning, the headmaster from his school rang.

"Jamie, I just want you to know that I and the staff are behind you. If you say you are innocent, then we believe you. You have been with us since you were fifteen; in that time, we have seen a boy turning into a man who is a credit to his family. When this is all over, I want to talk about your future. I will not see your chances ruined by this."

"Thanks, sir. That means a lot to me."

"Keep in touch, Jamie. If you need someone to give you a character backing, let me know."

"That was nice," his mother exclaimed.

*

Early the next morning, after packing, they set off for Manchester.

Jamie felt as if his old life had gone: no more drinking with mates, no studying, no going to the pictures in Edinburgh... A new life awaited, a strange life, an unknown one. Was that all he could look forward to?

And, strangest of all, he was together with his parents. Up until now they had skirted around each other. He had been farmed out ever since he could remember, only seeing them for a few weeks each year, before they were off again. He never really knew what they were doing – acting, yes, but what that meant he had never really thought about. Now he was about to find out. He would find out who and what were these two people that he loved so much.

As these thoughts ran around and around in his brain, he would have been surprised to know that those two parents had similar apprehensions.

"You know, John, we have to learn about Jamie in a different way. I suppose he has been a, sort of, on-and-off son. Now he is with us, do you think it will be alright?"

"Yes, dear," answered her patient husband. "He's a good lad. He knows we couldn't have gone off and left him."

"I hope he does. A new stage, maybe? We can be a family in every sense. Jamie has never grumbled or said anything, but it must have been difficult at times."

"We're a couple of old thespians; we have that bug called 'acting'. It doesn't work well with family life. But, yes, maybe this is a new stage. We love our boy, and he is more important than any play or ego-driven need."

"You are an old dear, John. I do feel something important has happened. It's strange, but all this is the stuff that drama is made of. The difference is that *we're* the drama."

They reached Manchester.

The apartment they had rented was in the city centre, not far from the theatre.

"You have that room, Jamie," his mother said. It was large and airy, overlooking the rooftops.

The lounge, while not very large, was cosy. But the kitchen was the best room, well equipped with every gadget you could want.

"What we do, Jamie, is divide the cooking. Maybe you could do the shopping; I can make a list each morning."

"Okay, Mum, that would be fine. I don't mind cooking, either; you've always encouraged me."

"So, you know what happens: the cast have a get-together in the theatre, before beginning to rehearse. After that, you could come and watch. I think it would be good to have a routine, don't you?"

One thing Jamie didn't want was to be aimless. "Maybe I can do something? Dogsbody? Cleaner? Stagehand?"

"Yes, darling, we can find out as soon as they are used to you being there."

When settled, they all went out to eat.

Jamie hadn't spent time with his parents for such a long time, and he was surprised to find that he liked them. *Really* liked them. They were well-read, charismatic, impulsive, loving and, so far, he had realized that, rather than finding their company boring, he was fascinated to find that he had two interesting parents.

The next morning, they were to be at the theatre by ten o'clock. "Come with us tomorrow, Jamie. That gives us a chance to let the company know you are here."

After lunch, they went off and left Jamie to walk around the city, to get an idea of where he was. Manchester was a bigger place than he realized.

Wandering around, he came across their theatre. There, on a poster, were his parents' names. The play was a new one, a light comedy.

Jamie had strange feelings. There he was, nearly seventeen, and he had never even seen or been involved in his parents' lives. All that he had ever wanted was alien to them; they had never understood and it had never been discussed. They hadn't talked enough. In fact, they had never talked.

"I can change that now. Understand them more."

He was growing up quickly, because of circumstances and unforeseen events: Jeannie and what she had done; and, just when he needed them, his parents – Mother a more than charming, though rather spoiled woman, and Father not the old-fashioned stick-in-the-mud Jamie had always thought he was.

He did a grocery shop, getting in essentials and filling the small freezer with ready-made food; he bought plenty of vegetables. Knowing they would be back at six, he started preparing dinner.

By the time they got in, there on the table were glasses, with a good wine, the table set and aromatic smells filling the flat.

"Oh, how lovely, Jamie!" his mother cried.

"Should have done this years ago," smiled John.

After dinner, over a coffee, it was suggested that Jamie could do something to help them.

"We are still memorizing our lines," his father said. "It would be such a help if you could hear us."

"That would be fun. Gosh, I never thought I'd be doing this for you."

"You might change your mind after a while. We're finding it a bit harder these days to get our brains to stick."

"Okay, say when."

"How about right now? Here is the script. It's a light comedy with tonnes of innuendo."

They settled down, with Jamie on one chair, and his mother and father together on the sofa. Jamie had never done this before. Whatever plays his parents had done all their lives had been a mystery. For the first time, he began to realize what this business of acting was all about. And, as they read through, to hear how professionals worked.

His mother's was a slightly dipsy character. Her dialogue was full of typical theatrical quips, which she delivered with gusto, using a tone of voice slightly in the style of the old melodramas. The male character was a comedian; hearing his father's delivery had Jamie in stitches.

"Now let's do it without the script. The only way, Jamie, otherwise we will never stop looking."

They started again. It ended with shouts and laughter at the mistakes – mostly Linda muddling up pronunciation of the word "magnamosity".

"There's no such word!" John exclaimed. "Magnanimous, maybe, or magnanimity. but 'magnamosity'? Definitely not."

"Well, *I* like it," insisted Linda.

"Maybe that's the humour of the play: putting in words that nobody knows," Jamie said.

The next morning, Jamie went with them to the theatre.

He found that the cast – a mixture of various nationalities - were pleased to meet him. It was a close-knit group. He could see that they had bonded in a short time. And both his parents were popular.

The rehearsal began – and pretty rocky, on the whole; some knew the script, some didn't.

"My god, we'll have to do better than that!" yelled the producer.

"Don't worry, this always happens," whispered Linda to Jamie.

In a break, he was introduced to the producer, John Smith.

"Good to have you with us, Jamie."

"I'd love to help out, if you need any bottle-washers."

"Better than that: how'd you like a part? Non-speaking? We had a lad but he's down with flu; can't play anything. You might enjoy it."

"Gosh, I'd love to!"

It turned out to be the part of a boy who delivers newspapers.

"Just open the door and throw the paper in."

"I'll need to rehearse, get my lines right," grinned Jamie.

"So, we have a new family thespian, do we?" John laughed, when he heard.

"Now, don't upstage us, will you, darling?" cried Linda.

"What does that mean, Ma?"

"It means that you never move so that the actor speaking has to look upstage. The biggest trick in the book."

"Wow, there's a lot to know." He began to think that this might be fun.

And the rest of the cast were, too.

"You're our lucky mascot, dear," they told him.

He found that actors are very superstitious: never wear blue; don't wish anyone luck; just say "break a leg"; and no whistling in the theatre.

"What on Earth do all those things mean?" he asked John.

"They're mostly ancient superstitions, still used. Acting is something that needs a crutch; it's a state of mind, hence 'break a leg'. To wish anyone luck is not on."

"On the continent, it's 'merde', which actually means 'shit'," laughed Linda.

At the next rehearsal, Jamie had a shot at his small part.

"That's it, Jamie: when you hear John say, *'Where's that bloody newspaper?'* you open the door and throw it in."

This is a doddle, thought Jamie. *I don't know why people make such a fuss.*

"Just wait until you have dialogue," laughed John.

The playwright was hovering about. A rather precious chap, who tittered and grumbled, running up and down, from the stage to the back. He had a shock of bright-red hair, tattoos on every arm and, to Jamie's amazement, wore lipstick.

A first day with plenty to do. Jamie thought that maybe this would be an interesting journey into the unknown world his parents inhabited. Funny how he'd always slightly despised their life, and now he was getting his first taste of it, beginning to see that it had attractions.

And he was, he grinned to himself, and actor too, now. A hypocrite, who had made judgements about something he knew nothing about.

The weeks passed and he was given jobs to do: making the tea at the breaks; helping the stagehands with the scenery... Every evening, they all had time together, playing Monopoly or Canasta. He was finding out what fun his new people were. He had never laughed so much.

Sometimes he wondered what Alix was doing. Had he gone ahead with his plan to trap Jeannie? Would he get into trouble if he was caught?

CHAPTER FOUR

After Alix had left Edinburgh, he had time to think about his plan.

Had he been mad to suggest it? It was a long shot, worth a try, maybe. That girl couldn't get away with it; Jamie was his cousin and his best pal. Planning, that's what he must do; a set-up. At least give it a try.

Getting back, he holed himself up in his bedroom and thought about how to do it.

Firstly, he must find a small, portable recorder. How? Who did he know? The local hi-fi shop! He knew the son of the owner, Johnny. If Johnny wanted to know what he needed it for, he could make up some excuse.

Next morning, he sauntered over to the shop, where Johnny was helping his father out in the school holidays.

"Hi, Johnny. I'm needing a small recording set-up for a party, to have some fun with. Is there one in the shop?"

"Not that I know, Alix, but I have one. You could borrow it."

"That would be great."

Bit of luck! Alix hadn't much spare pocket money.

"Could I have it soon, and return it the next day?"

"Sure. Hang on a minute, I'll go and get it."

When he came back, he showed Alix how to fix it up. It was so small it fitted behind Alix's lapel.

"Thanks a million, Johnny. I'll look after it."

Now came the difficult bit: how to meet Jeannie and not look suspicious. If she had seen him with Jamie it wouldn't work. He'd have to take that chance.

The next morning, he stationed himself at the far end of the town square. It was pretty busy, with workers crossing and criss-crossing. No sign of Jeannie.

He waited for over an hour. Then, just as he had decided to give up, he saw her in the distance.

Now that it was happening his heart went a bit faster, and he had a dry mouth. *Come on, Alix,* he told himself, *try to look normal or she'll suspect something is up.*

He waited until she had reached the other side. She was only a few yards from him. He walked out, looking the other way, and they bumped into each other.

"Oops, sorry," he exclaimed.

"That's alright. No harm done."

Alix was a good-looking boy. Would Jeannie take notice? Just for a moment, he thought she was about to walk away without a glance. Then, turning, she gave him a smile – a smile that had every invitation a young man would want.

Alix could have made a move then, but good sense told him that it would be better to wait. He smiled back and walked off, leaving her staring after him.

So far, so good. She was intrigued. Jeannie was not a girl who got many rejections. She had been attracted to this boy and he had walked off.

*

Alix returned to the square the next morning. He had not slept very well.

"Are you alright, Alix?" his mother had asked. "You're looking a wee bit peaky."

"I'm fine, Ma. Needing to catch up on schoolwork for next week."

He sauntered across the square. Would she be here again? Yes, there she was. Waiting for someone? He caught her eye and waved.

"Well, hello, there."

"Hello, yourself. Fancy meeting you again."

"I'm on holiday; not much to do. How about you?"

"The same, really."

"Would you like to go somewhere? There's a good film on."

"Well, I don't know. I'm not supposed to be picked up by strange men," she smiled.

"Let me introduce myself: Alix, at your service."

"In that case, yes, Alix, I'd love to."

"Okay, I'll get tickets. How about meeting at five o'clock, outside the café?"

He'd done it: first part of the plan achieved. Now the difficult bit: to keep it up for the whole evening and not make her suspicious.

He phoned Jamie.

"It's on. Pretty easy; this kid is an open book. Fingers crossed I can get a recording. I know she might decide she doesn't like me, or someone tells her that I know you, which would scupper it totally."

"Take care, Alix; this kid is no child. But, if you can do it…!"

He was waiting for her when she got there at five. She had put on a short, almost transparent dress, her hair curled and fragrant, long legs bare of stockings, with high heels which lifted her up almost as tall as Alix.

"I'm really looking forward to the film."

"Me, too. Come on, let's have something to eat first." He had borrowed some funds from his mother, saying he owed it to a mate.

She was good company, he had to admit: flirtatious, talkative and knew how to flatter a man. Barely sixteen, she had the manner of a mature woman. He hoped she wouldn't find him boring; he wasn't by nature a talkative person.

In the cinema she sat close, brushing his leg as if by accident. He could smell her scent: a delicate rose mixed with freshly washed hair. She was desirable, he couldn't help thinking. *Watch out!* he told himself. *Remember Jamie. Don't be a fool.*

Would she play the same game? Or had she decided he was not interesting? Well, he'd soon find out.

The film ended.

"That was great," she yawned.

"It sure was. And great to be here with you."

"The same for me."

"I'll walk you home. Are you far?"

"It's the other side of town. Thanks, that would be nice."

Walking side by side, Alix decided to do it now… or never. He slipped his arm around her slender waist. She didn't push him away, but just moved closer.

"That's nice, Alix."

He put his hand inside his pocket to turn the small mic on.

As they walked along, not speaking much, she said: "Would you like to go somewhere nice?"

"Sure. Where to?"

"Come with me."

She pulled him into a lane – a dark, silent, slightly damp-smelling lane. Halfway down, she turned and kissed him.

"That's nice. Do you like it, Alix?"

"Yes, Jeannie. Where are we, though?"

"I'll show you. Somewhere that no one ever goes to... at least, not at night." She pulled him into the graveyard.

Alix began to get cold feet; this was all exactly as Jamie had said. *This girl must be stupid,* he thought. She was playing right into his hands, doing something that was being recorded, leaving her exposed. Alix felt sorry for her – he couldn't help it; by what she was doing, she had lost the case.

"Come on, Alix." She stripped her dress off, lying naked in the moonlight.

"What do you want me to do?"

"There's a silly boy! What do you think? Don't you want what you see?"

"Jeannie, why are you doing this? What about Jamie?"

She sat up. "Jamie? What do you mean?"

"Meaning that I have a recording taken of the last ten minutes; this is all on it. That's why I made sure I met you yesterday."

She sat up, putting her dress back on. Now she was crying. "That's a dirty trick. I'll get my own back. You wait." She got up and ran, weeping and furious.

Alix sat for a while. He'd done it – more successfully than he could have dreamed of. He'd saved his cousin, yet he'd ruined a girl's life. Young though he was, he knew that what Jeannie had become was deeper than it seemed. You could just call her a crazy, mixed-up kid, but it was more. At sixteen she had become an experienced seducer. Alix shuddered.

CHAPTER FIVE

Alix rang Jamie early the next morning.

"I've done it. Believe it or not, she behaved exactly as you described."

"My god, Alix, you're a wizard."

"I'll come over to Edinburgh, talk to your parents and see what we should do. Main thing is to let the lawyer know."

"Okay. Say when and I'll get the train."

Jamie went to his parents. They were in the dressing room, being made up for the performance. He told them about Alix.

"Darling," cried Linda, "what a friend is that!"

He rang Sally. When she heard, she gave a whoop. "We've got her! Mind you, the recording might not be allowed; I'll have to find out. If it's done without the person's knowledge, it might be unusable."

"But it wouldn't have happened if she knew. That's a bit of a conundrum."

The next two days were free for his father and mother, while Sally talked on the phone, setting up a meeting.

"Doesn't this make a difference?" John asked.

"It sure does, though it depends on the judge, of course. Personally, I think there will be no need to take it further. Let's get this Jeannie and her parents to meet us, play the recording and see what they say. I would think they would rather drop it and save their child's reputation."

John suggested: "Well, what about Jamie's reputation? The press has already given it headlines. He has to be exonerated. After all, none of it is his fault. He's the victim."

"Let's call a meeting with the judge, play the recording and let Jeannie's parents hear it. Then an announcement can be put out that Jamie is innocent."

It took two days to get the judge to agree.

Jamie called Alix.

"I'll come over in the morning. I've managed to get the chap who loaned me the recorder to let me keep it a few days more. See you then, Jamie."

The meeting was arranged for three o'clock in the afternoon. Jeannie's parents were called and Mother came in, full of antagonistic belligerence.

Just you wait, thought Jamie.

"I really don't know what this is all about," said Jeannie's mother, sitting with her arms crossed.

Father sat uncomfortably beside her. He had never said a word from the beginning.

Jeannie was looking frightened. When she saw Alix, she turned white.

Sally asked the judge if she might speak.

"Of course, my dear. What do you have to say that might influence this case?"

"A lot, Judge. A recording has come to light that is directly concerned with it. A recording proving that Jamie Lindsey is innocent."

"Can we hear it?"

"Yes, I have it here."

"Right, please play it."

Sally put it on the machine which was linked to the loudspeakers. Into the quiet of the room came the voices of Alix and Jeannie.

Her voice rang out, clear as a bell: "Do you want to go somewhere nice?" Alix asking where; the kisses and the invitation; then Alix asking what she wanted.

"Silly boy. Do you want what you see?"

Then Alix telling her what he had done. Her anger and tears.

It was harrowing stuff. Jeannie sat with tears pouring down her cheeks. Her mother had turned almost purple. Her father shrank as he sat.

"This is a set-up. That's not my daughter!" Mother yelled.

"I'm afraid it is," Sally answered.

The judge sat silent for a moment.

"This changes everything," he said. "And you have a decision to make," looking at Jeannie's parents: "you can go ahead with your accusation, which is obviously not true, go to court and have your daughter shamed, or drop it, with the agreement that an announcement is given to the press that Jamie is totally innocent. It's your choice."

Jeannie's mother sat there, battling with what to do.

"Well, I can see that it was all quite different than I was told. I agree. We agree."

"A wise decision, Mrs. Macdonald. And may I also suggest that

Jeannie," looking at her directly, "has some counselling? What I have heard today has disturbed me."

Jeannie was beyond listening. Her cheeks were red with shame. Alix and Jamie watched with distress.

"I also suggest that this should be done with the minimum of talk and exposure for your daughter, Mr. and Mrs. Macdonald. There is no need to ruin her reputation in her community, but she must learn that she can't behave as she has done. Can I have a promise, Jeannie?"

"Yes. Yes, sir. I'm so sorry!" she sobbed.

"I will now officially notify the courts that an agreement has been reached. The parents have withdrawn their accusation and Jamie is totally innocent of rape, or anything else."

They left. It would be nice to say that Mrs. Macdonald apologized, but she was never going to. She just flounced off, dragging her husband and daughter, parting with a venomous look at them all.

"Looks like Mum is to blame as much as Jeannie," remarked John.

"I think so," agreed Helen. "But now we must contact the press, after the judge has done his part, and tell them the good news."

To Jamie, a load had lifted. He looked at Alix. "I can't tell you what a great thing you did for me."

"Och, Jamie, I'm just happy it worked."

"Let's hope that it all settles down, and Jeannie has learnt her lesson."

"Well, as I live in the same town, I agree. But I guess we won't become bosom pals!"

*

Jamie slept on the train back to Manchester. Relief was too light a word; he felt as if a huge load had gone. Yet, ironically, he still felt sorry for the girl who had nearly ruined him.

And, little though he knew it, something was developing that would change his life.

He could now get back to his old life, but he still had his promise to his parents and his part in the play, which he was enjoying. He now had, to his surprise, a pretty good idea why his parents loved the acting business; he was beginning to like it himself. So much that, at night, he lay awake wondering why he suddenly had odd feelings that the thought of being a doctor suddenly felt no longer attractive.

Everything had soon settled down again.

Then, one day, his old headmaster rang him. The papers had done a good job of announcing that Jamie was innocent.

"We are all so pleased and relieved, Jamie. When will you come back?"

"I guess as soon as the play is over, sir."

"That's fine, Jamie. Let me know. And good luck."

"Thank you, sir."

He had been doing his small newspaper-boy spot now for two weeks. His parents were a success. There was something about an audience – their laughter, their applause – and the camaraderie between the actors that was compulsive, and unnervingly potent for Jamie.

And he had almost made up his mind about something. He didn't want to share it with John and Linda yet – not until he was sure it was what he wanted.

For as long as he could remember, he had wanted to be a doctor; all of his studies had been based on that. Then, by accident, things had changed, making him realize, to his consternation, that in him were actors' genes. And, more importantly, that he loved it.

Was he good, though? He needed to know. How, though? His parents would be biased. So, who to ask? The producer might be an idea, but he had not shown any interest, other than giving him the small newspaper-boy part. What about one of the other actors?

On the other hand, could he trust his parents? Biased they might be, but they were professionals and they knew the game.

I'll try them first. See their reaction.

At dinner that night, Jamie put it to them.

"Mum, Dad, I need to talk about something. Firstly, I'm really enjoying the play – so much that it's making me think. I know I've always wanted to be a doctor, but I have to admit that I've loved the play – even just my small part. I never thought I could feel as I do. It's mind-blowing. So, what I want to tell you is… Could I be an actor? Is that crazy? Am I good enough? Do you think I have the ability?"

John and Linda, for the first time in their lives, were speechless.

"Darling!" cried Linda. "We would love it."

John looked at his son. "You ask are you good enough? That's something you must find out. The newspaper-boy role doesn't give you any opportunity. What you want is to get advice from someone who is not emotionally involved. I know just the chap. Would you be willing to gen up on something: a speech, some Shakespeare, or something you like...? I could help you, and let this man decide if you have it or not."

"Yes, Dad, that's just what I thought. If he was to say, 'forget it,' I would. It's just that I have found I am loving it."

"You know, Jamie," his father went on, "although the newspaper-boy bit you had in the play lasted only a minute, I will say, without bias, I did see something. But, because I thought you would never want to act, I never gave it a thought."

"Thanks, Dad. What I never realized was how dedicated you all are."

His mother smiled. "It's what drew us to it all those years ago. But, Jamie, it is so important that you give it time, to be really sure. It's a different life from the one you would have as a doctor.

"Tell you what: for the next run, the play will go to Eastbourne; we'll be there for two weeks. You can see how you feel then. It's in a lovely little theatre on the seafront. We've booked a hotel outside town, in an old village – Alfriston, I think it's called. So, while you decide, would you want to come with us?"

"I think I would. That means I'll have to leave school altogether. I am not sorry, really, as I lost most of my friends because of the Jeannie affair."

"You were amazing about that," Linda said. "It must have been terrible."

"It was. Much worse, though, if Alix hadn't ridden to the rescue."

"That boy's a hero."

So, plans were made to start the ball rolling.

Jamie went to bed, to dream of standing on a stage reciting a monologue from *Hamlet*.

When he woke in the morning, his first thoughts were: *I'm a doctor turning into an actor. Am I mad?*

CHAPTER SIX

As the days passed, Jamie began to wonder if he really was mad.

How long had he wanted to be a doctor? Why had he decided to be one? Had it been a rejection of his parents and their life? Was his change of mind because he had seen that the actor's life had attractions? He had to be sure. It couldn't be a passing whim. It was his future.

His father had asked a colleague to listen to Jamie. That would be the test.

"What are you thinking of preparing for Jonathan to hear?"

"I thought maybe something Shakespearian. Then, I reckoned that I am not experienced enough for that – especially reading to a professional."

"All Jonathan needs is to see how you put something over; you don't need to show that you are Laurence Olivier yet. How about something from *Hamlet*? There are several speeches that might suit. I'll dig it out." He rummaged on his bookshelf. "Here it is. Now, there are several great speeches; the one used for auditions is the famous one. On the other hand, you are very young, so maybe something more modern."

"I'd prefer that."

"How about Oscar Wilde's *The Ballad of Reading Gaol*? It's interesting – rather grim, but flows well. The start, *'He did not wear his scarlet coat, for blood and wine are red,'* is strong stuff.

"Can I try?"

"Let's see if I have it." He searched the shelves. "Yes, here we are." He looked at the verses. "How about starting at the section, *'Yet, each man kills the thing he loves...'*?"

Jamie had never done anything like this. He felt very exposed. Studying it for a while, he began. The words were descriptive; very graphic. "Shall I give it a go?"

"Yes, a first run-through."

He began. As he read, the drama Wilde had put into the poem began to fire Jamie up. Soon he had forgotten his father was listening – until he came to the bit, " *'Nor feel upon his shuddering cheek the kiss of Caiaphas.'*

"How was that, Dad?"

"Not bad. Slow it all down a bit; feel the drama; live it. Become that man." John said nothing more. He had been overwhelmed with what Jamie had done, realizing with astonishment that this son of his was a natural.

They worked on it a bit more, but John didn't want to lose the spontaneity that Jamie had shown on the first reading.

His colleague, Jonathan, arrived at eleven the next day.

Jamie, by then, was paralytic with nerves. Why had he agreed? What made him think he could act? Would this man just laugh at him?

"Hi, Jamie. I'm looking forward to hearing you. Just relax; I won't eat you."

Jamie began. Soon he was forgetting the man was there. How he loved those verses: the drama; the words that described the awfulness of the prison; the hanging; the knowledge that Wilde had been incarcerated in the prison. Jamie tried to think of these emotions as he read. He finished...

Silence fell.

He didn't know what to say. *Was I that bad?*

"Well, Jamie, you want my opinion as to whether you could become an actor?"

"Yes, I must know."

"In that case, I can tell you that not only could you consider becoming an actor, but I sense that you could be a very good one – with the right training."

"Really? Gosh!"

"If you do decide to give it a go, I suggest RADA. I can introduce you to the right people. Let me know."

After Jonathan had left, they all sat looking at each other.

"That was encouraging, darling."

"Yes, Ma... Although, I can't see what he liked so much."

"*I* saw it, Jamie," John interrupted. "It's that unseen *something* that not all actors have, difficult to describe. I guess it's a born thing, and you seem to have it."

"I was sure he would say I was rubbish."

He and Alix phoned each other every day, and Jamie let him know what had happened.

"Och, Jamie, sounds great. Give it a go. I'll be in the first row when you get there."

*

If Jamie thought that the rape case had died down, he hadn't reckoned on the media. Emails, phone calls, Twitter and Facebook messaging all wanted to know more. Who was the girl involved?

"Just give it time. They'll lose interest when something else comes up," John advised.

They had to think, as well, about money. Although, as the case never came to court, the cost of hiring Sally was minimal. She had become a friend of the family, just pleased it worked out. But, now that Jamie was thinking of changing career, it was financially different; his medical training would have been paid for by the state, but three years at RADA would not come free.

"Maybe we could find a patron," Linda suggested.

"Let's see if he can get in first, then maybe something could be found."

In the meantime, the company was going down to Eastbourne the following week.

At the last performance in Manchester, the producer came over to Jamie.

"I understand that you are thinking of being an actor. I have noticed you, and wonder if you could take on another part in this play, when we go down south?"

"Wow! I'd love to. What part is it?"

"It's the young man who keeps forgetting everything, and turns out to be the son of the character your mother is playing."

"Yes, it's a great part! But what's happened to James, who was playing it?"

"Hs mother is very ill. He feels he must be with her."

"Well, in that case, I'd love to."

Could he do it? Things were moving fast: one moment a doctor, going to medical school, the next on the boards, in his first real role on stage.

"That's a bit of luck, Jamie," his father said. "It will be good if you want to get into RADA. They like you to have some experience."

"Can you coach me? I have watched the part, so I know more or less what to do, but some help would be great."

"I'll take you through it. Now it's *our* turn to hear your lines," he laughed.

CHAPTER SEVEN

So much happened in the week before going to Eastbourne that Jamie felt he was not given enough time to think, far less learn his lines.

Jonathan, good as his word, had spoken to the head of RADA, and Jamie had an audition set up for December, giving him time to think about things, see how he got on with his small part in the play and have some coaching.

His aunt and uncle in Montrose phoned.

"We hear you are following your parents into the acting world. Well, my boy, that's a far cry from the respectable world of medicine," said Uncle, forgetting that he had aired doubts about whether Jamie was up to being a doctor.

"I think that's wonderful," his aunt said, unusually defying her husband. Jamie could hear his harrumphing in the background.

"Thanks, Auntie. Love to you both."

They seemed to have forgotten their horror when Jamie was accused of rape.

"Must have been difficult. You know, Pa, what I learned from all that was how quickly people condemn and judge before knowing the truth."

"Always been like that, I suppose. I agree, though, it's a shock when it affects you."

Now he had something else to think about: a small part in the play.

He didn't have to take over the role until Eastbourne, giving him breathing space. Every morning there would be family script-reading sessions, and Jamie began to get into the character.

"It's mainly about how this boy has discovered who his mother is. It's not high drama; it's black comedy, in a way, with lots of innuendo. But, at the same time, you have to show that you have found a long-lost mother. A difficult balance."

Always at the forefront of his mind was Jeannie. Not that he wanted her to be; he would rather have forgotten her completely. But, because of her all this was happening, and he worried about her. Stupidly. Why would he, when she had nearly succeeded in ruining his life? In a way, he felt guilty. It felt unfinished – he couldn't say why. Always in his mind was how she was. Would that beauty go to waste?

He and Alix still spoke most days. Alix wanted to be a policeman.

"Still hoping to be a detective one day."

"You seem to have a talent," laughed Jamie, "if your sleuth work on Jeannie is anything to go by."

"I see her occasionally. She's working in a shop in town."

"Does she seem okay?"

"Difficult to know. I heard that her mother threw her out. Nice woman, huh?"

"Maybe Jeannie learned something from it all. Let's hope."

"Yeah, you're right. How's the acting thing going?"

"I'll audition in London in December. Right now, I've been given a better part in the play. Isn't it daft, Alix? I never knew that acting was what I wanted to do all along. I just closed my eyes to it."

"I can understand. I reckon one of the best things to come out of the whole sordid business of Jeannie is that it made you realize you wanted to act. Life is weird at times."

"You can say that again."

The final Manchester season came to an end, the company disbanded and a rehearsal in Eastbourne was announced.

"Day after tomorrow, everyone. See you in the Devonshire Theatre at ten-thirty a.m."

The Lindseys went by car, travelling down the motorway and onto the A30, reaching Dean's Place Hotel, in Alfriston, in time for dinner.

"This used to be a smugglers' village," Jamie said, after perusing a leaflet.

"It's lovely," Linda answered. "So quiet after Manchester."

"Do you want to run through the part once more, Jamie?"

"Wouldn't mind. I think I have it, but some more wouldn't hurt."

After dinner, they sat in his parents' bedroom and Jamie read it through, without the script.

"How is that?"

"Why not do it again, with movements? Pretend you're on stage."

He tried again.

"Now, Jamie, let's do our scene together."

"Okay. I come from off-stage; you wait for my cue – *'Is that Robert?'* – then enter."

Linda looked at Jamie. "If you would have told me a month ago that I'd be sharing this with you I would have laughed. You can't know what it means to me."

"Me, too, Mum."

"Right, off we go. I'm on stage, talking, asking what's going on; cue: *'Is that Robert?'*"

Jamie came on, tripping over a chair – all part of the humour; a form of slapstick.

At the end, John said: "You did that fine. When you trip, practise it so that it looks a bit more spontaneous. Otherwise, you'll do. Now it's getting out there and doing it."

Next morning, they went into Eastbourne, finding the theatre after asking directions. It was tucked away, just off the seafront, a charming relic from the past. Small and not that well fitted out, it had the atmosphere of an old-world past that was attractive.

Jamie shared a dressing room with the other characters. Linda and John had their own. For the first time in his life, Jamie was sharing backstage banter.

As the son of the two main players, there didn't seem to be a problem. If any of them were jealous or resentful, they didn't let on. Jamie knew that, had his parents not been well known and part of the company, he would never have had this chance.

His test was soon to come. For the first time in his life, he would be on stage, in a play, doing a part, becoming an actor. It made him grin: becoming an actor... How did that sound? He liked it. He exhorted himself to keep confident.

Stay positive; it's only two pages. Remember what Dad said.

The bell went and he joined everyone on stage. The producer welcomed them.

"I know we have done this play now for a season, but, as you know, we have a new member of the cast: Jamie."

Everyone clapped.

"So, what I suggest is that we cover the scene with Jamie and Linda."

No time to think. In at the deep end.

Heart thumping. Dry mouth. Quaking.

Would it have been like this if he'd become a doctor, he wondered? Would seeing his first patient have made his heart go faster?

"Okay, start."

Linda began her scene and Jamie watched, listening for his cue.

"Is that Robert?"

As it came, he lurched onto the stage and, if his falling over the chair was intended, it was more because his legs were trembling. But he got through it and the rest of the cast applauded.

Had he been okay, then? Maybe next time around he could take more time. He felt he had rushed it.

"Jamie," the producer called him over. "That was a pretty good first try. Relax a bit more; it will get better."

"Thanks, Robert. I'll try."

They went through it again, then tried some other scenes.

"That wraps it up. See you tomorrow, everyone."

The theatre had set up the scenery and props, and the theatre director came down to say hello, while Jamie sorted out his costume: a suit with a waistcoat. It was a modern-era play, so anything would have been suitable.

Jamie had mixed feelings about it. He knew – or thought he knew

– that he had made the right decision. But he hadn't anticipated the nerves.

"They get better," John assured him. "Sometimes you always have them. They say Laurence Olivier had them every time he acted."

"You get that adrenalin rush, darling," cried Linda.

"Did I do okay?"

"For a first go, fine," said John. "You'll settle in, begin to put your own mark on it, add some bits… It's quite funny and you're nearly there."

What Jamie didn't know, and his parents were not going to tell him, was that he was being talked about. Not his acting, but his looks. At seventeen, he had grown out of the boyish, adolescent, gawky look, becoming an outstandingly handsome young man. Had he been told, he would have roared with laughter. But his parents knew it was an asset that would help him.

"Must have got it from me," laughed Linda.

"Course he did. Doesn't look like me – except maybe my eyebrows."

"He's got character good looks, not pretty ones. Pretty ones can be a disadvantage."

"Agree."

"You know, John, it's astounding that, after so many years rejecting what we do, he wants to be an actor, too. And strange how it came about. The power of the stars, maybe?"

"I know what you mean. Let's not crowd him, though. Parents are alright, as long as they keep their distance."

*

The performance day came too soon for Jamie. Evening arrived and time to go on.

And now an added thing to make the nerves worse: an audience!

He remembered what John had said: *Think about it. Concentrate. Become the character.* But supposing he missed? Tripped and fell flat on his face? Or, again, maybe that would be funnier?

Curtain up. The play began.

John had some good scenes, delivering the lines with experienced comic timing. Linda played her part like an old-fashioned, retired Hollywood actress; showing the inner pain, she felt for a son who was lost.

Jamie stood at the side, watching, listening.

Then: *"Is that Robert?"*

He entered, tripped and fell flat on his face. The audience roared.

"It's me, Ma!" he cried. *"Don't you know me?"*

It went like a dream from then on. Jamie delivered his lines and didn't forget one word.

At the end, he had his first curtain call.

"Bravo!" someone shouted from the back.

"Well done, darling," whispered Linda.

He'd done it! One up, ten to go.

Afterward, the cast gathered in a pub next door, where some of the audience came over to tell everyone how much they had enjoyed it. Jamie liked the bonhomie, the happiness of actors after a performance.

"Should have entered left side, not right," grumbled one small-part actor. "Really threw me. Good for you; keeps you on your toes."

The next day was free.

"Don't feel you have to be with us, Jamie. Get out and see the town."

"The boys have asked me to join them, to go to a disco."

"Go and have a good time. You've deserved it."

Alfriston offered few delights for an energetic, seventeen-year-old youth. He wanted some action. He got a bus down to Eastbourne, walking around to see what sort of town it was.

Nothing like Edinburgh or Manchester, this was an elegant, provincial, Edwardian town with stylish houses – mostly rentals – and shops. Plenty of charity shops. A sign of the times? He liked it. The seafront had colourful flowerbeds. The pier had just been restored after a fire, its golden turrets shining in the sun.

He was still in a delightful haze, after the euphoria of last night: those first cheers, that lone "Bravo!", until coming down to earth.

Okay, a small success. I have to do it all again, and a matinee on Saturday. Dad warned me: a learning curve.

It sure was. He grinned.

CHAPTER EIGHT

He had arranged to meet up with the others in a bar. They'd told him the name, with vague directions, but he had to ask, finally finding it down an alleyway. They were all there.

"Hey! Hello, mate," they shouted, as he walked in.

Jamie had only got to know them backstage, and then just briefly; here was a chance to spend time with the people he was working with.

Henry, the stage manager, was garrulous, middle-aged and overweight, with a never-ending flow of optimism and good nature, giving the impression that he was laid back to the point of making Jamie wonder how things ran so well – until he realized that Henry was meticulous in his way of doing things.

Then there was Anne *("with an 'e', please")*, a sassy girl of maybe mid-thirties. She was Linda's dresser, a rebel with strong opinions which, when she had a drink too many, became loud and argumentative. Jamie wondered if she was younger than she seemed. With cropped hair, thick make-up and large, round earrings, she looked more like a French gamin – something, although he didn't know it, that she was aiming for.

The leader of the group appeared to be Noel. He prided himself on being a personality. His job was looking after props. His voice was the loudest, and tonight he was in full swing. Grey hair, slicked back, hid a bald patch on a round, rather big head. His stomach was generously large – not surprisingly, as he swigged beer in copious amounts. "Welcome, Jamie," he bellowed.

They seemed to accept him. They could have called him "mother's darling", perhaps resented his elevation in the company – "Easy when you have influence," they could have said, and maybe they thought it – but Jamie didn't sense that. He mucked in with them, asked their advice.

"You're okay, Jamie," Noel said, putting a friendly arm around him. "Wasn't sure at first; wondered who you were, why you had joined us. But you're okay, mate; one of us. You are doing fine."

A bit later, the producer, Robert, joined them. Jamie was surprised, thinking he would prefer to keep a low profile, rather than joining the workforce.

"Well, hello, all," he called. His voice was a high falsetto which, together with his dyed-blonde hair, tattoos, earrings in abundance, topped with a variety of colourful clothes, rather puzzled Jamie.

What was more disconcerting was that he seemed to favour Jamie.

Henry took Jamie aside. "Listen, matey, you are pretty green in this game. There are all sorts of pitfalls and temptations. I am thinking you have not come across gays as yet?"

"I suppose I have. Not given it much thought, though."

"Well, beware: you're a good-looking boy and you will draw them. I say no more."

Jamie got his gist; he wasn't so innocent. But he was young, and so far he hadn't come across many gays, which he couldn't say worried him. One of his schoolfriends had seemed interested in questioning his sexuality, but it wasn't talked about among their crowd. Jamie didn't know or worry about what temptations lay out there. At least, he grinned to himself, Jeannie had given him a small idea.

The next weeks were a toughening of resolve and experience. More and more he felt, in his gut, that this was what he wanted to do. He now had ten performances under his belt; none had gone badly, some better than others. He was learning, trying different things. He liked to look at each new performance differently, keeping to the script but making a few changes. He watched the other actors; how did they do that? And he realized, very soon, how good his parents were.

The end of the contract came. Reviews had been good and Robert was pleased. Now what? He had until December to audition, so how to fill in the time?

"I'll get a job, to give me some money, and spend free time preparing."

"Good idea, Jamie," John said; "if you have a job, that will help with expenses. I am waiting to hear from Jonathan about the audition, so we know exactly what's required. I was going to suggest that we can spend time getting an audition piece ready, coaching you. Mother and I don't have anything booked in, so we're free. That is, if you don't mind."

"Gosh, no, Dad. Lucky to have your help."

CHAPTER NINE

Back in Edinburgh, Jamie did some jobhunting. There wasn't much going and he had no qualifications; all he could get was a job as a waiter. He ended up in a Polish restaurant in town. He wasn't a very good waiter, but he got better. The owner, who was also the cook, put up with a few disasters from him, such as dropping soup over a client.

John thought it all good experience.

"Use this to collect ideas: how people walk, how they react... It will come in handy one day."

So, he began to watch. There was plenty of material.

The Polish "aristocrat" (or so he told everyone) who came in every day – a tall, sallow-faced man with an abundance of white hair – would march in, order the same dish every day (called "bigos", a mixture of bread and sausages), and knock it back with a small vodka. He would bring his Polish newspaper and read it, emitting grunts and exclamations. He stayed just one hour, not a second more. His dress was old and stained, and too big, as if he wore it from a long-gone time. He looked distinguished.

Maybe he is from some aristocratic dynasty, Jamie fantasized.

Then there was the little old lady who trundled in, looking like a bag lady. Jamie wondered if she was someone famous in disguise. Her attire was made up of several layers of indeterminate clothing, topped by a man's hat, on a mound of straggly, grey hair. Her teeth were a dark yellow, three of them missing. Her eyes were keen, under long, grey eyebrows. Jamie was puzzled by her. She had a crystal-clear, upper-class accent and seemed to have plenty of money. She left Jamie a big tip every time she came in.

One day he would remember these characters, using them to enrich some stage character.

A woman he got to like was a writer. Elegant, well dressed, her dark hair in a chignon, and intense, blue eyes behind thick-rimmed glasses, she would sit and write in a large pad, observing people as they came in, making notes. She began to confide in Jamie after he had shown interest, finding this handsome youth sympathetic. She had several books published. She began to grow interested in him.

"Good luck, young man. Maybe you'll be a star in one of my filmed books."

The owner of the restaurant had a young daughter, Olga. At just fifteen, she looked to become a beauty one day, with her big, dark eyes, curling, black hair and budding figure. She hero-worshipped Jamie, which embarrassed him. He was understandably wary these days.

After he had been working for about a month, the owner invited Jamie to a birthday celebration at his house.

"It is usually just family, but my daughter asks you come."

That weekend, Jamie took a bus out to Cramond. The house where his boss lived was a large, rambling, typically Scottish house, set in an overgrown, rather wild garden. Inside, a huge fire glowed at the end of a spacious, comfortable room.

Jamie was warmly welcomed. He sat next to Olga in the dining room, at a vast oak table loaded with food.

It was noisy, everyone talking at once. These Poles knew how to enjoy themselves.

The restaurant owner, Aleksi, was an exuberant, larger-than-life, very friendly man, sporting a luxurious, black beard and moustache. Today he was intent on enjoying his birthday. Dinner over, he rose to make toasts.

"To my birthday. God bless my Matko and God bless you, Ojeciac."

"That is my grandmother and grandfather," whispered Olga to Jamie.

"I give you toast, my friends. Drink the vodka. Eat. Drink again. Eat again. You never to get drunk." Aleksi roared with laughter.

Jamie liked these people: so spontaneous, warm and passionate.

Working in the restaurant, he learned a lot about Polish cuisine, which, to be honest, he didn't like: a heavy, fattening mixture of sausage, sauerkraut, beetroot, cucumber, sour cream, mushrooms and more sausage, as well as smoked sausage.

He worked three days a week; the rest were free.

He organized a coaching itinerary: two hours after breakfast, then an hour each afternoon. John had received the audition requirements from RADA. They made interesting reading.

"It says here," John said, "you must be eighteen, speak English and have intellectual, creative ability. And this is very interesting: if you entered for the BA with honours in acting, you might be able to join for free."

"Wow! Now, that *would* be interesting."

"There is also the Conservatoire, in Glasgow, which does acting courses, but RADA is obviously the important school of acting.

Incidentally, you don't have to audition in London; there are regional places."

"Do I need A levels?"

"It does say five, with specific subjects."

"So, that means staying at school and getting the A levels. That's okay; I would have had to do that for medical school."

"Let's take it further, see your headmaster, work things out."

"I could keep my job; earn some income, too."

"Maybe, but let's see. The fees are nine thousand pounds a year, but there are free places. Again, let's find out more."

"We have talked about it, Jamie," Linda added, "and we want to use our savings to fund you. You can look upon it as a loan. That's only if you can't get any financial help; we earn too much for a free place, I think. And, anyway, what's money for? And there's another thing: we have a great friend who lives in London; if we offered some rent, maybe you could board with him and his family," Linda told him.

"Mum and Dad, you are fantastic. Okay, you could help me, but I don't want to take your savings. If it comes to that, we could draw up a proper agreement that says I return whatever you put out for me, as soon as I start earning enough."

"Now, there speaks the boy who wanted to be a doctor and finds maths exciting! Alright, darling, that's fine."

"Something else: why RADA? Can't I learn to act in, say, the Glasgow Acting Academy? I believe there is one. Then I don't have to live in London. I can pop home at weekends. Costs will probably be nothing like RADA. I have read a bit about it; it's very difficult to get accepted, and I'm not certain if that's the way I want to go. I just don't know."

"That's a thought, Jamie."

"I'd like to get some good A levels, as well, just in case it doesn't work out. There must be hundreds of would-be actors out of work – I wouldn't want to be one of them!"

"Didn't know I had such a practical son."

"Go on, Jamie."

"I'd like to take another year, get my A levels, then go to Glasgow."

"You will still be only nineteen," John said; "it makes sense."

Jamie felt in charge, at last. The thought of using his parents' savings didn't sit well with him.

The next day, he contacted the head at his old school.

"That would be no problem," Mr. Mackenzie said; "I can put your name down for the next term. In the meantime, come in, Jamie; we can see which subjects you will want to cover."

Things seemed to be making sense.

Jamie's time in the company had begun to have dreamlike qualities.

"Am I too practical to be an actor?"

What Jamie couldn't have guessed was that a letter was about to arrive. One that would alter his life.

"Dear Mr. Lindsey,

"I am a film producer in London, and I am writing to find out if an idea I have might interest you. I saw you in a play in Eastbourne last month. I am looking for a young, unknown

actor for a new film; I thought you could be suitable. I am looking for a young man to take the part of the son of the main character.

"Casting starts in the next few weeks. If you are interested, please ring me on the above number and arrange to audition.

"George Alexander."

"Now, that's interesting," Linda commented.

"Acting in a film?! I've had no experience."

"Sometimes that can be a good thing, you know, Jamie. Many actors never go to acting school. Your mother and I didn't. Most of our friends didn't. You can learn as you go. This is a good opportunity. Why not go, audition and see what comes out of it? Remember those young actors who were in the *Lord of the Rings* trilogy? They had no experience. Younger than you, true, but it can be an advantage; no preconceived ideas."

"In that case, I will."

He rang the film producer.

"Great, Jamie! Glad you got back. I'll send you the script. Gen up on the part marked, and come down to the studio when you're ready. Let's go from there." He rang off.

Surely he was dreaming? Only two months ago he was planning a career in medicine; now he was going to London to audition for a part in a film!

"If that isn't surreal..."

"That elusive thing, luck, plays a big part in life, particularly in our game," John said. He glanced at his son. "Maybe this is yours, so go with the flow. If it doesn't work out, put it down to experience; you can still go down the acting school road. If it does, then you will have been handed a start most young actors would jump at."

All very well, thought Jamie, *but, audition?! In London?!* And what sort of part was it? Would he be in Regency costume? A sort of *Downton Abbey*? Was he up to it? Did this commit him, no turning back?

The script arrived two days later. His part was marked out; opening it, he found he had a name: *"Young Son"*.

"What should I get ready, Pa?"

"Let's find a section where you have a lot to say," John replied, turning the pages. "Look here: almost a page without interruptions."

"Guess I'd better read it through, get an idea of the whole script and see where my character is in the story."

"It looks interesting. I've looked up this chap and his company. He's well thought of and has had some successes."

"I guess I'd be an idiot to turn this down, wouldn't I?"

"True. Why not look at it as experience, going into it with the attitude that it's not a life-or-death thing? And, as Mother says, what is there to lose?"

That night, Linda and John talked over what had happened.

"You know, John, I watched Jamie in Manchester. He was good. Not experienced, but the seeds of what might come were there, don't you think?"

"Yes, I saw it, too. It's a hell of a difficult decision for him. After all, only a month ago he was going to be a doctor. He has time on his side, but I believe he can do it. We know what makes an actor. He's young, full of energy, and offers like this don't grow on trees. He'll work out which way to go. Most of all, deep down he must want to do it."

"Well, I wish I'd had that chance at eighteen; for us it's been a slow journey. And there's the income; will he earn enough?"

"If he gets this part, I'd say yes. You know, Linda, how did we produce such a handsome son? And clever, too?"

"Of course, it comes from my side."

"Naturally, dear."

For the next week, Jamie worked on the audition. The following month, Linda and John would be leaving, as an offer of a play in Birmingham had come up.

"Let's see what can be done before we go."

Jamie was given some audition tricks, including the technique of playing to a camera.

"Try to avoid looking into it, unless there is a moment when looking right into the lens seems relevant; that can look strong," John suggested.

"Don't get too tense. Easier said than done, I know, but it shows. Every eyebrow lift, every change of expression, is blown up on camera. Don't overact; be yourself, or how you think the character would react! And, above all, don't be intimidated by fellow actors! They want the job, too, and some won't be kind. Just think positive and believe you can do it. It's not the end of the world if you don't get it."

"Thanks, Dad. I think I have some ideas. The part seems a bit passive; he's a nice guy, but has he any bite?"

"It's interesting you say that. What you might find, if you get the part, is that the producer will develop the role as the film goes along. If the actor can prove that he has more interesting possibilities, he will see it."

After a few more days, trying different approaches and finally committing it to memory, Jamie rang the producer, to tell him he was ready to audition. He was given instructions about where the studios were, and a time.

A family friend, who had a flat in Kilburn, offered to put Jamie up. So, on a Tuesday, getting an early train, Jamie set off.

"Ring if you have news, darling," shouted Linda, as they saw him off at the station.

"Will do, Mum. 'Bye, Dad. Thanks for everything."

John and Linda watched until the train was out of sight.

"Well, my dear, in a week's time our son's life might change."

"I know. Or he'll be back here. I shan't sleep until we hear from him."

"Yes, you will! Never the day when you don't go off in a minute, to snore all night."

"I don't snore! Look who's talking."

"Anyway, he's off and I have a good feeling about it. You're right, though: I will probably wake up thinking about him. He's entering a bear pit. Let's hope he can cope."

CHAPTER TEN

Jamie arrived at his parents' friends in time for dinner, after getting the tube across London, knocking on the door, with its slightly worn-looking paintwork.

It opened to reveal a large man with a face brimming with welcome. He lifted Jamie's suitcase in, at the same time shaking hands.

"Well, hi, Jamie. It's great to have you with us."

Michael, a warm, rather cuddly, overweight man, exuded bonhomie. Jamie learned during dinner that he worked for the BBC as a cameraman.

"Have you done any camera auditions?"

"I've never done any auditions anywhere," Jamie admitted.

"If I can help, just ask."

His wife, Mary, was the complete opposite of her husband: angular, electric-blue eyes and an intense gaze. Jamie wouldn't know it, but she would become a warm and staunch friend. She was an artist; her paintings covered most walls: lurid, highly coloured, very modern, in-your-eye creations.

"It's great to have you, Jamie. Your parents are such good friends; to meet you, too, is a real pleasure. Last time we saw you was when you were, I think, about three. We were impressed by how your mother carted you around theatres, and how well-behaved you were."

"Wouldn't say I remember. Maybe that was when I got the bug and didn't know it. Jolly nice of you to give me somewhere to stay.

By the way, I have to be at the studio, for the audition in Bayswater, for ten o'clock. Any idea how long it will take?"

"Give yourself an hour, to be safe. If you get there too early, you can always have a coffee somewhere to steady your nerves."

"Which I'll need."

"You won't be alone; don't forget, all the people auditioning feel exactly the same."

To his surprise, Jamie slept well, waking in the morning looking forward to the audition, which surprised him. He thought about being a doctor: that first patient; the aural exams, when he would have to tell an examiner why he wanted to be a doctor. No different, really – or so he tried to convince himself.

He got to Bayswater with about twenty minutes to spare, and had coffee in a little café, letting his heart slow. "Deep breaths," John had advised; "calms the nerves."

Then it was time.

He went across the road to the studio, where inside sat a long line of young men, all about the same age. Were they there for the same role?

"Don't think negatively," his father had said.

"Okay, Dad, I'll try." But it was tough not to be intimidated.

He sat down. No conversation, just tense silence.

One by one, they were called in. He was the last.

"Jamie Lindsey, please."

"Yes, that's me."

"Hello, Jamie, great to see you. Now, don't worry about the camera; just do your thing. We need to see how you come over."

Everything he had prepared seemed to vanish. Total blank!

No chance, not with all those people looking and assessing. His father's voice rang in his ears: "Go for it, Jamie! Remember you are good."

Taking a deep breath, he began. Tentative at first, until he forgot the people listening and watching. He *became* that young man.

Right at the end, he turned and looked straight into the camera. Not blinking; holding the moment; ending with the final sentence.

Silence. Nobody in the room moved.

Okay, he had failed. He was useless. They hated it. He might as well go home.

Then he heard a voice: "We've found our Laurence."

Had he heard right?

"Jamie, you are booked. You have the part! Terrific. Bravo.

"We'd like to talk about terms; time schedules... Your scenes will be in one or two sessions. I want to see how we can develop your part. You may not know it, but the camera likes you."

"No, I didn't. Is that good?"

"For a film actor, yes, very. And, something else you'll have to do: Equity will be onto you. I am assuming you haven't joined?"

"No. My parents said something about that."

"Look, we know that you haven't been doing this for very long. That's one reason we asked you: you're an unknown, a fresh face. We'll take care of everything. You may need an agent, although I wouldn't hurry. We can talk about fees between ourselves. There are

Equity levels of pay."

"Thank you for choosing me."

"Let's hope you enjoy it. We have a good cast lined up; you'll meet them soon. They are a good lot." The producer then reeled off some names, mentioning a very well-known actor. "Filming won't begin until everyone knows what they are doing. Can we contact you easily?"

"I'm staying with some friends in Kilburn. Here's the number."

"Great. Well, good to have you. Thought you might do when I saw you in Eastbourne."

"Gosh! Glad I didn't know!"

"Jamie, you are a natural. It's all there. What you have to find is technique, that stuff that supports you on the off days. You can get by with natural talent, but stagecraft comes with experience, which can be a vicious circle: to get experience you have to have it."

"Two months ago, I wanted to be a doctor. Now, here I am, trying to be an actor."

"All that might be useful. It's a funny old world, theatre: when it works, it's a potent, absorbing art form. Learn, Jamie; collect experience. See what we can make of you in your first film role."

Jamie left the studio. Walking on air. Totally shattered. Not quite believing. Why had he been chosen? Maybe he would know if he could see the filmed audition. What had they seen that he couldn't?

Getting back to the flat, he let himself in with the key that Michael had given to him. He phoned his parents on his mobile.

"Guess what."

"You got it!" Linda cried.

"Yes. They were really nice, giving me all sorts of advice. They want me to join Equity, and talk pay sometime later."

"Jamie, we can come down to help, if you want," John called. "Don't want to mollycoddle you, but you are now in a new world, and it needs to be done carefully. You should get an agent; that's something you will need. We've got an honest one, who's a friend. Would you meet him?"

"I don't know, Dad. I've still got to get my head around the whole thing. By the way, your tips sure helped me. The producer told me the camera liked me. Does that mean anything?"

"For a film actor, that's gold. Take it a step at a time. Learn how to use a camera, then later how to project on stage. The techniques for acting on film are totally different to acting on stage. Less is better than more."

That night, Jamie fell into bed and slept without waking.

First thing he thought in the morning was: *I'm a film actor. How daft is that?*

He was being swept along, into a crazy new world of actors and producers.

"Come on, Jamie, forget analysing. Go with the flow," his father had said. But it was happening so fast. He needed time. Time for what? Wheels were turning. Exciting? Yes, he was young enough to be caught up in the euphoria.

Next day, the studio called.

"Come and meet everyone tomorrow, Jamie. We want to talk terms, get a contract ready." They gave him an address. "See you around ten a.m."

Jamie called his parents again.

"Dad, they want to talk terms. Maybe I should have a word with your agent. I haven't the foggiest about pay."

"Let me give him a ring."

Ten minutes later, Jamie was talking to the agent, Mark.

"Being your parents' agent has been a privilege, Jamie; to have you as well would be great. Can we meet up this evening, before you go to the film crew tomorrow?"

"Can you come here? It's quiet, and I'm sure the people I'm staying with won't mind." He asked Michael and Mary if that was okay.

"Of course, Jamie. Tell you what, let's all have a meal, then you can talk about what you want after."

The agent arrived on the dot. Letting him in, Jamie liked what he saw: quite young, around forty, with a dark beard and moustache. His smile warm and genuine.

Mark saw, when the door opened, a very young man. *My god, he's handsome.*

"Hi, Jamie. Great to meet up like this."

"Ditto. I think I need help. Let's go in. Michael and Mary have suggested we all have a meal together, then leave us to talk."

Over a meal in the dining room, where Mary's paintings looked overpoweringly down on them, conversation ranged from the art world to the acting profession, the jungle that Mark worked in every day.

"It's getting more difficult," Mark said: "less care taken of young actors. Thrown into any old T.V. sitcom – easy fame – then disappearing overnight."

"How can that be avoided?" Jamie asked.

"Shouldn't say this – sounds arrogant – but to avoid it you need a good, honest agent who understands the pitfalls."

"Ma and Pa seem happy. I guess that's good enough for me."

Alone with Mark, he had questions.

"Jamie," Mark interrupted, "let me tell you what I can do. I can put you up for Equity. I can negotiate your fees with the company, get a contract up and running. In other words, I can take care of things that would be tricky for you, then you don't need to worry, especially as you are new to this game. All you will need to do then is concentrate on the job. For all that I take a twenty percent commission. I never sign away an actor's freedom to change agent, but so far I haven't lost anyone."

"I guess that takes care of my worries. I was beginning to feel that so much was happening and out of my control."

"Think about it, Jamie. Let me know."

"I don't have to; I'll sleep better knowing all that side of it is being taken care of. Will you take me on?"

"Will do. Welcome to the Mark Rylands Agency."

"That's excellent news," John said when Jamie rang, after Mark had gone. "We've been with his agency for all our career. We started with Mark's father and then Mark himself. He's a strong, supportive chap, and gets us some good gigs."

"I liked him. This means I can concentrate on the part. I'm meeting the cast tomorrow; I'll let you know what it was like. Let's hope they treat this new boy okay!!"

"Of course they will, darling," cried Linda down the phone.

"Just be yourself," John added.

That's all very well, Jamie thought, after putting the phone down, but who was he? He should be himself? Well, what had he done? Nothing. Many great actors were playing Hamlet at eighteen, and he hadn't even started.

Up early the next morning, Mary put a good breakfast down. "Must eat, Jamie. Stoke up your energy."

Should he dress casually? How would the others dress? He decided on jeans and a jumper, with a jacket, trying to see in the mirror how he would look.

"What do you think, Mary?"

"Hmm, about right: casual but smart. Maybe a shirt, rather than a jumper; it'll get hot in the studio."

In the end, he decided on a shirt and a jumper, dropping the jacket. He was ready.

Mark rang just as he was leaving.

"I've spoken to the company. They will meet up with me and I'll take care of everything."

"Thanks, Mark. I'm just off. Wish me luck."

Getting to the film studio at ten, he found everyone was already there. Taking a deep breath, he went in.

"Hi, Jamie, come and meet everyone."

First one over to him was the actor playing the main male lead.

"Hello, new boy," he drawled. "Welcome to the bear pit."

Not very promising.

Jamie said: "Thanks. Good to be here."

He was joined by the female lead: a household name – small and blonde, with a kind, lively face.

"Welcome, Jamie. It's your first film, I understand?"

"Yes, to be honest, I'm pretty terrified. I will get used to it, I suppose."

"There's always a first time for everything. Let me help you if you get too stuck, or want any advice. You look a nice boy. I'll enjoy having you for a son," she smiled.

Gradually, he met everyone.

One girl, cast as a maid in the film, came over to him. "Hey, sweetie, how's a handsome kid like you got into this game?"

"It's a first, see if I like the game."

"I'll help you to like it, if you want, ducky."

"Thanks; best to get on my own. You're playing a maid, is that right?"

"Yeah. Well, them over there seem to see me as a servant. I wanted the sister role, but no way; that bitch over there got it."

He was getting into deep water here.

Just as he moved away, the producer called the whole cast together.

"Sit down, everyone. Before we start rehearsing, I want to talk over the plot and your parts in it, and where we will be going. The plan is to make a series of around six episodes. This way, the characters can develop. Most of you know how I work: nothing set in concrete; storyline developed. Things can change as we go along, but I have an overall concept of where it might go."

"Who do you see as the main character, Robert?" the male lead, Jonathan, asked.

"I suppose, at this stage, the mother. In the book, the story tells about how she gave away her son for adoption. The son has been brought up by a couple of Scottish farmers. Jamie, your Scots accent will be part of the storyline."

Jamie had wondered about that.

"How the two meet is the main thrust. The father role is fairly passive until this lost son turns up."

"Okay, I'll buy that," the male lead, Nigel, commented. "Feel better now, Robert; my role had looked pretty boring on paper."

"Right, everyone, have a break."

He went over to Jamie. "Okay, Jamie?"

"Fine. Glad about the accent. I had been wondering."

"As I see your character: about your age, a farm worker; in the first shot, a handsome, bronzed, healthy-looking, young man."

"I'll try!"

"Your job is to reveal how, even though you are just a farm labourer, under it all is an intelligence. You are the son of an intellectual, so the part asks for that subtle change."

"I'll think about that."

"Use what I think are natural, instinctive reactions to the role. I hope your character will find things that might establish a direction.

By the way, your agent contacted me; a good choice. He and I will do the necessary."

"Thanks, Robert."

After the break, the whole company sat around, talking: grumbles aired, ideas suggested, plots dissected...

"As I see it," Robert finally said, "it's a story of redemption – a common enough idea: giving a child away; the mother, very young, unmarried, a victim of society."

As he spoke, Jamie remembered the story of a young, unmarried mother in the Isle of Lewes, put in the pulpit by the minister, to be shamed in front of the whole village, while the father sat among the congregation. He put that away for future reference.

Robert announced: "We'll take a two-day break, everyone. I have copies of the book; take one – please read it. Come back with ideas."

That suited Jamie. For one thing, he wanted to get up to Birmingham, to see his parents, talk it over with them, and to see the play they were in: Oscar Wilde's *The Importance of Being Earnest*. He was a new boy in the business; lots to catch up with, absorb the world he had entered. A junior player in an adult world of thespians and experienced players. At any moment he would be found out, come crashing down.

On the train to Birmingham, he read the book. He could see why Robert looked upon it as a series: you couldn't really say all there was to say in one film. He tried to imagine who this young man was, what he felt, especially when he met his real mother; in the first part, he had no idea she was. A lot to think about.

John and Linda met him at Birmingham New Street station.

"Darling!" Linda cried. "Wonderful you could come. We want to hear all about it."

They explained they had taken a suite in a hotel near the theatre.

"So much better than having to cook."

"Hope it's going okay down in London. Did you take on Mark?" John asked.

"He's taken on me! He's great. I'm now on his list. He is very fond of you both, by the way.

"Anyway, I'd like you both to read the book the film is based on and, if we could talk over ideas, that would be helpful."

"Right, let's get back to the hotel and spend the evening together. We don't have a performance until tomorrow, so you are our priority."

Their hotel was in the centre of town – one of those very modern, swish places. Their suite had three bedrooms, with a tiny kitchen, in case they needed it.

That evening, they talked through everything: what the producer had said; details of the other actors…

"You are lucky to have Judy as your leading lady; she's well-known for helping young actors," Linda told him.

"She's already talked to me: said she was glad to have me as her son!"

"I can just hear her saying that. I worked with her some years ago. Really enjoyed it."

How lucky he was to have these two people, who understood this new profession he had been thrust into. If he could go back to London with positive ideas about the character he would play, he would start with confidence.

Over dinner, they caught up with general things, keeping the main ideas until they were in their suite.

"Jamie," John started, "we have an idea. It's great that you have been chosen for this film but, on the other hand, you are new to the game. What we think you should do, when it's over, is to get a tour, out on the road, night after night. Mark has already said he could fix something. This film will help: give you some background; get you a good touring company."

"That's exactly what I was wondering. I need space to make mistakes."

"In a way, it's a substitute for drama school," Linda exclaimed.

"Have I made a mistake taking this film on?"

"It has positives and negatives. If it works out, you will have made huge steps in getting work. If it doesn't work, which I doubt, it will be an experience."

They had answered his worries, to a certain extent.

"I'll speak to Mark, see what he has in mind."

He got through to Mark the next morning.

"Hi, Jamie. Bravo getting that part. I've had a word with Robert; he's happy to have found you – thinks you are perfect to play the young man."

"Hope he's right. I've got two days to work out how to approach the role. By the way, Mum and Dad suggest that I go on tour, to get experience. What do you think?"

"I agree. Wouldn't be too difficult. And don't forget, if the film role goes well, I could probably find a really top company."

"I guess what I need is a year or two touring, learning new plays, finding out what it's like to be an actor."

"Nothing better: a great training ground. Most actors begin like that."

Now he had direction. A huge challenge. So much to learn. So many possibilities of falling flat on his face. But, excited? Yes.

The next day, Linda and John had a performance; Wilde's play was in a theatre in the city centre.

"Lovely to have you here, Jamie," Linda said. "You can be our critic. It's a play you could do one day, you know."

John was playing the Reverend Canon Chasuble, and Linda was the formidable Lady Bracknell.

"Edith Evans created a big problem for anyone playing Lady Bracknell: when she cries, *'A handbag!'* in that wonderful voice, no one else would dare to copy it."

"How have you decided to do it, then?"

"Pass it off as an aside, an exclamation, a puzzled query. It's a pity, for I'd like to do it as Dame Edith did it, but don't dare. It's too famous."

Sitting in the theatre that evening, Jamie saw how the mechanics of acting could work. Watching his parents on stage, for the first time, was a lesson in technique, something he knew he hadn't got. Not yet.

That weekend, he, John and Linda mulled over the book, throwing ideas around.

"It all depends on how your producer sees your part. You could go back with all sorts of ideas and he could throw them out."

"So, you think I should just know the story inside out, then let the character develop under Robert's direction?"

"That's all you can do. Ideas grow in a free, unscripted way. Remember that film *Casablanca*, with Bogart and Bergman? They say it had little direction but, when you watch it, it seems perfect."

The next day, Jamie returned to London. No going back. He was committed.

I'll let it all happen. Bloody lucky, I guess. So, go on, Jamie, don't muck it up.

Everyone had arrived when he reached the studio. He sensed a different atmosphere: a working one. Everyone was tense as Robert outlined the order of reading.

"Okay, folks, you have the script, you've read the book – I hope! – so let's just read through, get an idea of character. Let's start."

The opening scene was for the mother, setting the scene. We learn that she has mourned all her life for a lost son; flashback to illustrate. Jamie didn't have anything until the second scene. He just listened, taking it all in, watching the actors as they read.

"Okay, Jamie, second scene," called Robert. "You have no idea this is your mother."

It went well. Jamie had worked out what sort of person he was:

not well educated, but smart.

Breaking for coffee, Robert came over.

"That's the idea: the brawny, good-looking young man. A bit like that Bill Travers – remember him? Big-hearted, handsome guy, slightly dim in some ways, but a certain innocence."

"I get the idea."

For the next two weeks, every day was spent reading and discussing any ideas offered.

Wardrobe came in to talk about costumes; Jamie seemed to be given mostly farming outfits: thick shirts, dirty trousers... "Has to look as if you've been in the fields," Robert grinned.

The weeks flew by. Jamie knew now, without any doubt, that he liked this business of acting.

Mark contacted him to see how it was going.

"I suggest that you wait to finish this T.V. series, get the reviews, then I can approach a touring company."

"Okay, Mark."

"By the way, you do know that you get paid for these rehearsals?"

"So I gather."

"Union pay, per hour. Then, when it's up and running, you get more for things like repeats."

"Wow! I like this game."

And he did. Every week, a good sum went into his bank. He paid for his room at Michael and Mary's. They were full of interest and, every evening, at supper, they would talk over the day's shooting.

Jamie honestly didn't know if it was going well, but Robert seemed pleased. He was fitting in with the other actors. They were a happy lot, fairly laid back, generally, although few frustrations coming from the bit actors.

The girl playing the maid spent her breaks sliding up to Jamie, whenever she could.

"Come on, ducky, no need to be snooty."

Young he was, but not stupid. This girl was too blatant and dangerous, with obvious sexuality. Too much like another girl he had known. He was growing up in every sense.

He had his nineteenth birthday on a rehearsal day. In the break, a cake was brought in.

"Happy birthday, Jamie!"

After three months, the six episodes were nearly wrapped up. It had gone well. A tragic and moving story. Judy, the mother, was incredibly powerful. Jamie felt that he, too, had created a reasonable character.

"Jamie," Judy said, as the last day came, "you have done well. I would say you are going to be good and have a great career. I hear you are thinking of going on tour, to get experience?"

"Yes, I am. I need to feel free to make mistakes."

"Quite right, dear; the very best training you could have. That's how I started. But listen, if this series is successful and you get some good notices, don't be swayed by that; there is no substitute for solid touring, night after night, play after play."

"That's what Mum and Dad say."

"I know your parents; we did a play together."

"They told me. Mother loved working with you; she told me it was always fun."

"Funny old thing, life," she laughed. "Keep in touch, dear boy. Here's my address and email; let me know how you are getting on and, if you want any help, don't hesitate."

"Guess I'm unemployed now," Jamie laughed, when he was on the phone to his parents.

"You'll always have those times. Not too many, I hope."

He met up with Mark in his office.

"We wait now, Jamie, see how the critics are; quite a lot hinges on that. Silly, I know, but that's who the theatre people listen to."

"Should I sweat a bit?"

"Not really; just being in Robert's series is pretty powerful. Have you seen the rushes, by the way?"

"Yes, we had a session. Somewhat mind-blowing, actually, seeing yourself on the screen."

It had been. Had he come over as he thought? He couldn't have said; it was impossible to separate the person on the screen from himself.

"I think I got the character right, and I do think the scene with Judy, when I realize that she is my mother, was quite good."

"Robert seemed to think so. Anyway, let's wait."

Up in Liverpool, John and Linda agonized over this first job for Jamie.

"Suppose they say he was no good?"

"Now, Linda, darling, have faith. It has been a very difficult start for him; would have been better if it had been the other way round: touring then the T.V. chance. But let's see, our boy might be an overnight star. Who knows?"

"Oh, John, I hope so. We know only too well what an up-and-down job this is."

"Let's just be happy that our only boy is following in our footsteps. It's what we both always wanted."

"Okay, buster, I won't worry. Our son is going to do well."

The first episode was shown the next week. Jamie couldn't watch; he felt sick just thinking of it.

"I've got the papers," Mary called, before breakfast. "Come and look, everyone."

"I can't," muttered Jamie.

"Well, you should, dear. Let me read you a bit of it; I think you'll like it:

"*Last night, in the new series of plays by Robert James, a new star was born – a hunky young man that will set every girl's heart racing...*"

"Oh, my god!"

"There's more:

"*We understand this is his first job as an actor. If so, his future is certain.*"

"Wow, Jamie," Michael said, "that's pretty impressive."

The phone rang. "Darling, have you seen the paper? Fantastic, darling. So proud!"

"Yes, Mum. They must have been looking at another film."

"Now, Jamie, you've got it made; it will be all the easier for you. Mark will be over the moon."

Later that day, Mark rang.

"Great, Jamie; gives me a good chance to find you a really good company. This means you won't have to slog in some second-rate group. Believe me, that's a plus. I'll do some investigations and get back."

"Okay, Mark. Thanks."

Jamie now had free time. He decided to go over to Montrose, to see Alix. He needed to find a bit of peace and mix with normal people. Which made him laugh; he had decided that actors were not normal. Lovely, but not normal. Alix met him at Montrose station.

"Hey, great to see you, mate, star of television. Wow! Fantastic, Jamie."

"Can't believe it, really. But I'm not grumbling; so far, so lucky."

"Enjoy it, anyway. Great to see you."

"Me, too. Seems an age since we slouched around the square. God, remember that? How we first saw Jeannie? Whistled at her?"

"How could I forget?! I bump into her occasionally. I heard that battle-axe of a mother threw her out. So much for mother love! I've seen Jeannie around with some men. Can she change? Doubt it. She's intelligent and beautiful, but maybe it's too late."

Jamie went to see his uncle and aunt.

"Oh, Jamie, we read all about you in the paper yesterday."

"Just a flash in the pan, boy," grunted Uncle.

"Yes, Uncle, probably." He would never change; still led Auntie a dog's life.

While Jamie was in Montrose, Mark rang.

"Jamie, I've had a call from a touring company in London. They are off on a two-month tour next month, asked if you would like to join them."

"Do they know why I want to do this?"

"Yes, I've filled them in. They saw you in the film, and have ideas about which roles to give you. The play is a murder whodunnit. You might get the second policeman."

"I'll say yes, then. Thanks a million."

That night, he lay in bed, thinking.

Lucky, or did he have something? What, he didn't know; one can't see themself. In such a short time, he was actually off on this career. He would work hard, learn roles and find out what he was best at. Was he excited? *I'll say.*

"Apprehensive, yes," he whispered to himself, "but bloody excited."

He fell asleep to dream of standing on a stage, expounding monologues, none of which he had ever read. Waking in the morning, he realized that soon he might be doing just that.

CHAPTER ELEVEN

He had a month to prepare. The company sent a script to him; could he look at it and learn it, ready to start? There were times to join them, contact emails and telephone numbers. There was to be a month rehearsing. Michael and Mary said to stay with them again.

Back in Edinburgh, he went to see the Polish people in the restaurant.

"We knew one day you do well, our Jamie," laughed Aleksi.

It was good to be among these people again, with their zest for life. The owner's daughter, Olga, had married, at just seventeen; she seemed happy with her young Polish man.

Aleksi slapped Jamie on his shoulder. "Fancied you something bad, she did, me boy. I would have been happy. But we knew you had something to do. A man has to follow his star, don't they say?"

Jamie's first script was a play about a murder. As Mark had thought, he had the part of second detective. Not a big part, but important in the scheme of things.

"You'll be on the road for some time, Jamie," John told him. "It's a good idea to get some things that will be useful."

"Such as, Dad?"

"You'll be mostly in digs, not hotels, so something to make a cup of tea or coffee, and plenty of warm clothing when winter comes. All new for you but, I promise you, well worth it. A test of endurance, at times."

"Can't wait."

"Let's hope you come out the other end seasoned and tough."

Over the next few weeks, Jamie learned his part. He found, to his surprise, that he had a photographic memory. He stayed in the Edinburgh flat, only going out to eat and see friends.

His old headmaster rang one morning.

"Well, Jamie, a lot has happened since we last spoke. So pleased to read about the T.V. series; my wife and I can't wait each week to see what happens. Well done; we are all proud of you. Will you, maybe, come in and talk to the boys about what you are doing?"

"Yes, I would like to do that. Let me do this tour – I've a lot on my plate right now – and I'll ring you when I get back, around the middle of next year."

He still woke every morning in a state of amazement. Only a few weeks ago he was going to be a doctor. Already that seemed a far, distant dream. Would he regret it? Was he in this acting game only to find he was no good? To realize he had made a mistake?

"Maybe I should stop this questioning, like Dad said."

The time came to go to London and start rehearsals, taking place in an old house in Hampstead. For the first time, he met his director, Peter Hall.

"How do you do, Jamie? Good to have you with us."

Peter introduced him to the others. "By the way, I'm no relation of the great Peter Hall, in case you have wondered."

He was a giant of a man, with a large head of thick, grey hair. His dress was, as Jamie would find out, always a mix of artistic and casual.

A well-formed nose made up a face of character, rather fierce, brown eyes and a set of spectacles which perched, often precariously, on the end of his nose. He had a smile which, when he was amused, showed a mobile mouth with strong teeth, exuding merriment and a zest for living.

There were seven other actors. Jamie was the youngest.

"Hi there, Jamie. New to this game, I understand?" a craggy actor said, going over to say hello. "Never done a tour before?"

"No, I'm looking forward to it."

"First time can be fun. Can be a bit of a bind, though: home life and all that. James, by the way."

"Hi. Jamie."

Another actor strolled over. "Well, dear, you're a sight for sore eyes." The speaker, rather feminine, had a high-pitched voice, and was maybe five years older than Jamie. "Saw you on T.V., darling. Thought: *What a hunky chap.*"

"Do you think it came over?"

"I'd say so, darling. My name's Bob, by the way."

He was joined by a laconic older man. "Norman. Good to have you."

"Good to be here."

Norman was a chunky-looking man of around forty. Taciturn and solid-looking, Jamie learned that he always got the policeman sort of roles. He had a kind face and an attractive smile. "Just ask, if you don't know what to do. It's always tough at the start."

As he spoke, a woman glided over. Tall and magnificent, with dark hair swept up to a chignon, she looked Jamie over.

"Well, honey, saw you on T.V. You look younger in the flesh, but could see you are photogenic."

"Gosh, really? Hadn't thought about it."

"Very important in our business, honey. I'm not very photogenic; I always look too fat on film."

Jamie thought it best not to react to that, but he made a note of her name: Gloria. Well, that fitted!

"Okay, everyone, let's get going," Peter called.

They sat in a circle and began. Jamie was glad he had worked on the script; these actors were experienced. Jamie reckoned he held his end up.

His dialogue was fairly minimal, but the best bit in the second act, when he found a clue which led everyone to the murderer.

He met the actor who was playing that part. He had the look of James Mason: dark and sullen-looking, until he smiled. But good – very good.

By four o'clock, the meeting was wound up.

"Thanks, everyone. Good session. Call at ten-thirty tomorrow. Memory by Friday, then we can start marking."

As Jamie headed back on the tube, he looked back on his first day's work. Had he been okay? No one had said. But, for a first session, meeting so many new people and getting the hang of it, he felt reasonably pleased. A huge learning curve.

"It went pretty well today," he told John and Linda, when he rang them that evening.

"I'm sure it did, darling," Linda cried. "You're going to be just great."

"Take it day by day, Jamie," Dad said. The voice of reason.

Jamie smiled, thinking of his mother. Didn't mothers always think their children perfect? Still, if she didn't, no one would.

He went to sleep with dialogue running around his head, waking in his usual state of surprise that this wasn't some strange dream.

Rehearsal began as soon as everyone had arrived.

"Let's get going. And, just to let you know that we will be doing Wilde's *The Importance of Being Earnest* after this tour. Also, I have a list of towns, dates, et cetera, and names of theatres."

Funny how Linda had commented that Jamie might do this play one day, and now maybe he had the chance... or was that being too confident, too soon? Gosh, that would be a big one to take on. If Peter cast him, what part would he play, Jamie wondered? He had watched it in Liverpool. Algernon seemed a possibility. Or maybe just a footman!

After another run-through, Peter called: "Okay, everyone, let's try the first scene without scripts."

Jamie had just three lines in that scene. Peter organized where everyone would stand or sit; Jamie was told to stay by the door and wait for his cue. They went through it twice.

"Okay, not bad, everyone. Have a break, then let's look at the second scene." Jamie had more in that scene.

Peter came over. "So, you can establish a character, Jamie; decide what you see in your part. Maybe you could develop into a young man looking for love, or sex, or something – you know what I mean?"

"Sort of, Peter. I can see how easy it would be just to walk through the part and never make an impact. I'll think about it, try different things."

"Are you interested in the Wilde?"

"My parents were in it only last week. I sat through several performances. Loved it."

"I know your parents. Terrific actors."

"Thanks, Peter."

After the break, they ran through the second scene. Now Jamie had a chance to get into more meaty dialogue, and took the chance, after what Peter had said, to establish a link with the main female part, flirting with her a bit. She was a small, blonde actress, with a pert, snub nose and a wide smile. Taking the hint, she played up to Jamie.

"That's good," Peter called. "I like that reaction, Phyllis."

By the end of the day, they had set the whole play loosely.

"Better than I'd hoped. We'll do a complete run-through tomorrow, then get the costume people in."

"Like to join us for a drink, Jamie," Bob asked, "get to know everyone better?"

"Yes, sure, Bob."

Everyone, minus Peter, gathered in The Horse and Groom, down the road. "Everyone buys themselves – better that way," called Bob, which suited Jamie; he hadn't much money on him.

They were a colourful group. The oldest was Jean, a full-busted, rather loud woman, with a contralto voice which could pierce a sheet of metal. She rarely seemed to stop talking, whether anyone listened or not.

"Now, Jean, just belt up for a while, dear," Bob said. "You're not the only person here, you know."

"Well, thank you, Bob, dear. I will maintain a total silence from now on, if that's how you feel."

"Don't listen to him," James laughed; "you're lovely, dear."

Jamie was sitting next to Norman, who was playing the main policeman. Next to him was a skinny, black-haired actress, lips a gash of red lipstick, large, gold earrings, long, expressive hands and bright-red nails. She cast big-eyed glances at Jamie, leaning over in a lull.

"We must get together, dear boy. Tell me all about yourself."

"That's Fanny. Watch out, there; a positive Delilah she is," someone called.

Jamie tried to commit all their names to memory; he would be with these people for months. So far, they were nice; no resentment that he had been on T.V. Just a new boy, in their eyes.

At the other end of the table sat an extraordinary-looking person, Jamie wasn't sure if male or female.

Bob saw him looking. "Transgender. Used to be a man, but transitioned into a woman."

"Looks nice. How does that fit in with casting?"

"The funny thing is that she plays male roles very well. You'd never guess, but now she's up for the female ones."

"Maybe the victim? Or the murderer? Do we know who that is?"

"Not yet."

His parents had told him all this would be an education... well, it sure was.

"What's her name now?"

"She's called Francesca; used to be Frederick. She's rather nice, by the way. You'll like her."

What Jamie was discovering was that actors were not like other people; they acted *all* the time. It was a surprise, as his parents were not like that at all. Looking around the table, everyone was at it – maybe because they had just met, or because they had to make a mark right from the beginning.

I must appear very boring.

As if he had read Jamie's mind, Bob leant over. "This will wear off, dear boy. It's just the usual manoeuvres; always happens at the beginning."

"I had wondered."

Bob laughed: "Just stay as you are, dear boy."

That evening, back with Michael and Mary, they wanted to hear all about it.

"I love your description of them all," Mary laughed.

On the phone to Linda and John, Linda cried: "I know some of them. Jamie, you have a fascinating group, by the sound of it."

"Don't get too close at the beginning," John suggested. "Find out which ones are the least likely to make life difficult. There are always jealousies. Plus, you are young, and many actresses are on the lookout for a good fling in bed."

"Oh, John, that's a terrible thing to say!" cried Linda. "But I suppose you are right, if I remember rightly."

"Oh, really? Now you tell me."

"You know what I mean, dear."

"Come on, you two. And don't worry; I can look after myself."

CHAPTER TWELVE

The weeks flew. Then, at last, the play was up and running. Everyone seemed pleased.

Jamie had worked out what to do. His scenes went off okay.

"Thanks, everyone. Good work. Now, about the tour: you have the itineraries, so I'll meet you at the theatre in Nottingham. Also, have a look at the Wilde; I'm casting it next week. We can work on it at the location."

The cast had begun to divide up into cliques. Jamie found himself with Phyllis and Norman quite a lot of the time. She seemed to have decided to make Jamie her confidant, even disclosing that, in her first season, she had become involved with the lead man.

"Awful mistake that was, Jamie. In fact, it never works," she told him: "tempers start, jealousies, rivalry..."

"I can see that. What happened then?"

"Got into a real mess. Anyway, I want to learn to be a fine actress. I won't let anything get in my way."

"That's how I feel."

"Well, stick to it. You've plenty of time for all that."

First night came.

The Nottingham Theatre was a fine, old playhouse. Backstage was a bit basic, but nobody minded.

Linda and John came down. Jamie was shaking through the performance, but he managed to get on and do a decent job.

After, Peter took Jamie aside. "That was fine, Jamie. You just need to loosen up a bit, get familiar with the stage; it won't eat you. Otherwise, I was pleased."

"Thanks, Peter. That means a huge amount to me."

"You could play Algernon in the Wilde play. Only thing is the accent; any chance you could iron it out?"

"I'll give that thought, Peter. Am I ready, though? It's a different style."

"I have an instinct, Jamie, tells me you could do it."

"Can I think about it?"

"Of course. You've got to jump off the deep end sometime, and I can coach you, if you would like. You know, I have a feeling about you. Might be wrong, but I rarely am."

"God, that would be fantastic, Peter."

So, what had he learned so far? That you must own the stage. That there is an audience out there, watching every move, every speech.

He told John and Linda what Peter had said.

"He's right," John answered: "you must find that elusive level of relaxation and confidence. It only comes with practise and experience. Don't hurry – you have something; build on it."

"Should I take on the Wilde? Or is it too early?"

"It is a big one. That's the point of touring, though: you can fall flat on your face, learn your trade without major critics seeing you."

"Peter wants me to lose my accent."

"It would be an advantage. You know, of course, that we both did. Otherwise, there's always a danger of only getting cast in Scottish parts."

"Sean Connery managed."

"Not initially; if you see the early Bond films, he was obviously trying to sound more English. It was only when he became a big star that he no longer had to worry."

"Okay, Dad, I'll go for it."

"Why don't we go through it with you?" Linda suggested.

"That would help. It's a special style: sort of Wilde tongue-in-cheek humour."

"Hilarious, particularly when you read it."

Next day, the critics came out. They liked the play. Critical of the lead, but liked most of the actors. Jamie had a small mention: *"...new young actor who played the part of the policeman competently..."*

"That's a good start, Jamie. Not too much attention just yet."

Linda and John left the next morning; Jamie saw them off at the station.

"Just remember, Jamie, go with the flow, keep trying things. Proud of you, my boy."

Jamie went back to the digs; the whole company was lodged in a B-and-B near the theatre.

"This is pretty good, compared to some I've been in," Norman told him.

It was a house with a garden. The landlady was a great supporter of the theatre. "I like to have the actors stay, dear. Always stimulating."

She provided large meals, believing a good breakfast was vital for actors. "Gives them energy. I have to say, they are my favourites. I have opera singers here sometimes, as well. Noisy lot, they are, always warming up; scales from every room. Singing at you, as well. Gets on my nerves, I can tell you."

So, Jamie began the life of a touring actor, *"Like the troubadours of old..."*

What he hadn't realized was that the whole day would be free until performance time. So, he devised a plan: morning looking at Wilde's play, in his small bedroom, until lunch; a walk after lunch; then back to check on the evening's performance, making sure he had not forgotten anything.

Peter had suggested that he play Algernon, who would be a bit older than he was. Very wealthy, with tongue-in-cheek dialogue; a terrible snob, for whom it was normal to put down a servant. "Imagine the repercussions if you did that now!"

Even if Peter changed his mind, or thought him not ready, he decided to learn some of it. He practised a bit of the text, trying to lose his accent, lengthening the vowels, changing the shape of some words. It was hard going. He couldn't hear himself – that was the problem.

Everyone gathered for lunch at one o'clock.

Francesca sat next to Jamie.

"How do you do, Jamie? We didn't get a chance to meet in London. Are you enjoying it?"

"Hi, Francesca. Yes, okay so far. All very new to me."

"Saw you in the T.V. series. Thought: *There's a nice, new face.* Didn't reckon we'd see you on a tour, brave boy."

"Right, well, thanks. I got the T.V. thing out of the blue. Guess it's a good idea."

"Sensible boy. Yes, you are right: in the end, it will pay."

CHAPTER THIRTEEN

There was a performance every night and two on Saturday.

"You're right, Dad: it does toughen you up," Jamie said to his father, on the phone that night. "Every night, twice on a Saturday and I'm just in a small role. How do you manage with a big one?"

John laughed. "Stamina; build it up, particularly if it's an emotional part. Learning to pace yourself. Having a routine day to relax. All sorts of tricks you develop."

After the final Saturday performance, Peter called everyone to have a drink, and talk about the next place they were going to.

"Well done, everyone; it's gone well. Good critics, on the whole. I have also decided on the Wilde cast; I'll put it on the B-and-B's noticeboard, so you can see. We have a week free until our next place – Bath – so go off, take a break and look at the Wilde."

In the morning, the list was up on the board.

Jamie had read through the part of Algernon to Peter, and not very well, he thought. So, when he saw the cast list, he was stunned – and, if he was honest with himself, pretty scared at the thought.

He was Algernon.

Gloria was Lady Bracknell; Norman was the Reverend Chasuble; Bob was the manservant; Miss Prism was to be Fanny, doubling with Francesca; James was the butler; and Phyllis was Gwendolen.

Jamie stopped Peter as he was going out.

"Thanks for that, Peter, but can I have some time to decide? First of all, I have to think about my accent, and secondly, have I enough experience to manage such a lengthy role?"

"Okay, Jamie, we don't meet for a week. When we gather again, in Bath, let me know. I think you can do it, but I don't want to push you. There will be extensive rehearsals in London."

Jamie decided something: he had to get away. Be by himself. Concentrate totally on this new challenge. But, where? He hadn't a lot of spare cash. He had a bank account but, as pay went directly to Mark, he hadn't any funds right now. He rang Mark.

"I've been offered Algernon in Wilde's play. As I have a week off, before Bath, I want to get away and look at it. I've told Peter I would decide then. Thing is, I need money to get away somewhere."

"No problem, Jamie, I'll put your fees in your account. Great news. Hope you decide."

"It's happened so fast, Mark."

"Listen, Jamie, I've nurtured many young actors; you aren't alone. Go with the flow. You've made a great start – honest."

Everyone seemed to have more confidence in him than he had himself, right now. He knew what he should do: get away and work on his accent, then come to some decision about this mountain he had to climb. He had thought it through: aside from the Wilde play, if he wanted to tackle other parts, his accent would always be a drawback. But how to set about it?

"Listen to other people. Get recordings of Shakespearian actors. You don't need to lose all your accent, just the more extreme vowels and consonants," his father advised him. "Many actors have the ability to lose their real accent entirely; you can decide which way you want to go."

*

The next day, he set off, getting to Bath by lunchtime. It took him four hours of trudging around B-and-Bs before he found one that had a vacancy. Terms were reasonable.

"A bit more if you would want supper, young man."

"Yes, I would, please."

His bedroom overlooked a road with a line of lovely Bath terrace houses. He had a bed, a chair and a basin. Bathrooms were evidently shared. It would do.

He had a plan. First of all, he let Peter, Mark and his parents know where he was. Then, as he'd booked in at six p.m., after trudging around, he was starving.

A gong clanged, and going downstairs he saw people in the lounge: residents, he assumed. In the hall, a desk filled most of the space, where the landlady, Mrs. Jeremiah, sat in splendid and regal control: a large, statuesque woman of maybe sixty, grey hair piled up into a bouffant; heavy, dark-rimmed glasses on an aquiline nose, under which thin lips were a gash of red. She had on a gown with high, padded shoulders.

She's been watching Dallas, Jamie grinned to himself.

"Good evening, Mr. Lindsey. Supper will be served in half an hour. The lounge is through there. You can meet your fellow guests."

Jamie went into a largish room which had chintz curtains, chintz chairs and even a chintz footstool. Four people were seated, reading or watching the T.V.

"Good evening," Jamie said. Four heads looked up.

"Well, look here," one of the men answered. "What have we here, now?"

"I'm Jamie."

"Well, bully for you. I'm Willy."

Not an auspicious start.

"Take no notice," one of the women interrupted. "I'm Janice, by the way. Welcome to sunny Bath."

"He's always rude at first; it's sort of a game with him," the other man said. "I'm Jake, at your service."

"That leaves just me," the other woman added. "I'm Clarissa, and don't laugh at my name: Mother had just read a novel where the heroine was called Clarissa. I just have to be thankful that her name wasn't Delilah or Clorinda."

"We're the young set, by the way," laughed Willy; "wait until you see the other residents."

"That's rude, Willy; they can't help being old! Besides, I think Mr. Carstairs is a lovely man."

"You would say that, dear, just because he compliments you."

So far, Jamie hadn't spoken. They seemed nice, if a bit brash. Would they ask him why he was there? Of course they would. What should he say? Pretend he was on holiday? They wouldn't buy that: a young man all by himself?

"Can't get a drink in this godforsaken place," Willy said.

"There's a pub down the road," Jake replied. "We could all meet up after supper."

The gong sounded again.

"Like something out of a B movie," Clarissa commented: "the toll of doom has struck. Supper is ready."

Everyone laughed and went into the dining room, where the table was set for supper: sliced gammon, salad, and tea served from a chintz teapot, matching the chintz teacups and saucers. Someone liked chintz!

Already seated were three elderly people, including a couple, the woman thin and nervous looking, her husband a burly, red-faced chap, with receding hair and a belligerent look on his face.

"Come on, Mavis, set about pouring," he ordered.

"Yes, dear."

"How do you do?" Jamie offered.

"We do just fine, young man. I am Mr. Milward and this is my wife." All in broad Lancashire. "We're here in Bath to take the waters, just as they did in the old days."

"Good evening," said the other man, a person of maybe eighty, distinguished looking with a cheery, open face. Jamie liked the look of him. "I'm Carstairs, by the way. What brings a young man to Bath?"

"I'm touring. I'm an actor. I thought I'd come down early and see the town." It was the first time he had said that to anyone: "I'm an actor." It felt good.

"It's a beautiful one; I know the town well. I'd be pleased to tell you where to go."

"Matter of opinion," Willy snorted. "Just a load of old buildings, if you ask me."

"No one did, idiot," Clarissa snorted. "You are a philistine, Willy."

After dinner, Mr. Carstairs invited Jamie to sit with him in the lounge.

"I think you are here for a reason, Jamie," he asked.

"How did you guess?"

"I sense a purpose in you. You are, perhaps, nineteen?"

"Yes, I am. And you're right: I am here for a reason."

"In that case, I'm curious."

So, Jamie told him all about what had happened to him since the affair with Jeannie. This old man and his interest gave Jamie the freedom to talk about it. A friendly stranger.

"So, there you are and here I am, beginning a life in a profession that, three months ago, I had no intention of joining."

"Well, dear boy, this is fascinating. And, if my opinion will be of help, I am willing to give it."

"I'd love to hear it."

"You know, life is a strange mixture, with decisions to be made; we all make bad ones and good ones. A bad one at a crucial time can be a lifetime's regret; a good one can open a new world. My feeling, from what you have told me, is that it would seem someone out there thinks you have talent, and that has to be nurtured; developed. If you were my grandson, I would tell him to stick to it. You have time on your side, and right now I can guess you are at the crest of something that might very well be your life.

"As for now, you want to lose your accent. I think you are right to do this. But, look upon it as not losing that attractive Scottish burr, but learning to be able to switch into another voice when it is required."

"That's a help. I had wondered about that."

They stayed chatting until Carstairs went to bed.

"Old age gives me the privilege of retiring early without remark," he smiled. "If I can help with your work on your voice, feel free, Jamie. Goodnight, my dear."

To his dismay, Jamie realized he had not asked the old man about himself. *Just what I hate people doing, I've gone and done myself.* He'd make up for it tomorrow.

At breakfast next morning, the four younger ones were still bickering.

"What shall we do today, Jake?" Clarissa asked.

"I'm going to get drunk," Willy grinned.

"Oh, go off and get lost."

"I suggest we take a picnic and get out to the country," Jake interrupted.

"How bourgeois can you be? A picnic? Thanks a lot."

"Well, you needn't come."

And so it went on.

Mavis appeared. "Hello, everyone," she greeted them. "Lovely day."

Without her husband, she came over as a sweet woman with a lovely smile, which soon disappeared when her husband joined her.

"Get on with it and pour my tea, Mavis. Stop that chattering."

Jamie nearly shouted: "Pour your own."

This man was a typical northern bully. One of those blunt, arrogant men who enjoyed making people miserable and looked down on the opposite sex. It was a study to see the faces of the young ones as they listened. In their world, someone like Milward belonged to the era of the dinosaur.

Jamie had a good breakfast. He doubted he could afford lunch, so stoked up until the evening.

The young ones left and the Milwards finished, too, Mr. Milward dragging his wife off, his nagging voice ranting until they left.

Soon, Mr. Carstairs joined him. "Good morning, Jamie. I trust you slept well?"

"I guess so. Goodness, I talked too much last night; didn't ask about you. Why you are here?"

"I'm not very interesting, Jamie. I was a lecturer on Renaissance art until I retired, speaking at the Tate and Tate Modern for many years – a subject very close to my heart. I believe I was quite good at it."

"I bet you were. The only art I know is what I learned for my GCSE exams, then didn't carry on."

"Maybe one day: theatre, literature and art surely go together. I always felt that I was lucky to spend my life doing what I loved. You will find it one day, Jamie. We can't do everything at once, but life deals unexpected blows. I and my wife had intended to go on a long art cruise but, alas, she died last year. So, here I am, in Bath, trying to work out what I will do. You see, Jamie, what I said last night: decisions… life is just one big one, from start to finish."

"Bad luck about your wife. Seems so unfair."

"Well, that's another thing: you say it's unfair, but so many things are; it doesn't discriminate."

"Can I take you up on the offer to help me with my accent?"

"There, I knew I had a reason for coming here. I would love to," he smiled. "So, I suggest… what about a session every morning and afternoon?"

"Whatever suits you best."

"After breakfast for a couple of hours, then go out and practise."

"Okay. Today?"

"Good. And call me Donald, please."

They decided on Donald's bedroom, where there were two seats, and which was larger than Jamie's.

"Right, let's start with you reading something. Maybe from the Wilde play, if you have it."

"Yes, I've brought it."

Donald took it. "Let's try that first speech that Algernon has, so I can see what you've done so far."

Jamie read it.

"Right, basics. Vowels: longer than the way a Scot pronounces. Words like 'your': you say it more like *'yoor'*, whereas English is more like *'yohre'* – a longer vowel, more open."

So, the morning passed.

Jamie struggled, though gradually getting his tongue round the words. Donald was a good teacher.

"Right, Jamie, that's enough. Now go out and find people to speak to. Practise some phrases."

That was more difficult than it sounded; English people take a while to open up. In Europe, if you sat at a dining table with strangers, they would talk, greet you, wish you a happy meal. Not here; only if invited. So, Jamie decided that's what he would do: invite conversation.

He walked around for a while, ending up in a park. He sat down where three people were sunning themselves.

"Good morning."

All three turned and looked.

"Good morning to you," one of the men said.

"Are you local people?" Jamie asked, in what he thought was his best English accent.

"Yes, we are. We live just across the road. What part of Scotland are you from, then?"

Well, that hadn't gone too well! He had a long way to go.

"It's early days, Jamie. Don't be impatient," Donald said at supper.

For the next five days they worked. Gradually, Jamie unlocked his voice, beginning to sound different; an intellectual exercise of moving slowly away from the sound he'd had in his ears all his life.

He felt he was coming on when he met some people in a café and they made no comment about his voice.

"Do you think I am English?"

"Why, yes, of course."

"I'm a Scot, actually. I need to lose the accent for a part in a play."

"Well, we couldn't tell. Good luck with that."

He couldn't have got this far without Donald's help. They had become friends. This old man had given him something rare: a quiet and studious certainty that anything can be achieved if you work at it.

"I'll be at the play, Jamie. And let's keep in touch; I am so interested in your progress."

*

On the Saturday, everyone assembled in the Theatre Royal.

"Welcome back, everyone," Peter called as they gathered. "Rehearsal this afternoon, two p.m. sharp."

Jamie was nervous. Tonight he was going to try his new accent. Should he? Shouldn't he? Surprise everyone? He might fall flat on his face!

Rehearsal came. It was now or never. Off he went.

Nobody laughed. Or said anything. Didn't they notice, then?

Peter had.

"Well, Jamie, I don't know how you've done it, but you have."

"Thanks, Peter. I think it's getting there."

"I'll say so. Bravo. It was my one reservation. That's why I mentioned it."

"It's been a struggle, but glad you noticed."

"Tells me a lot about you, Jamie."

"By the way, I'm lodging at a B-and-B in town; came here a week ago. I'd like to stay on there, if that's okay."

"Fine, I'll make a note of the address."

The performance was at seven-thirty. Jamie had time to get back to the B-and-B, have a bath and a bite to eat.

The four young ones were back, too.

"Just discovered you're in a play, mate," said Willy. "We're all going."

"Oh, Jamie, ever so thrilled we are. Someone famous and all," Clarissa trilled.

"I'm not that; just beginning, really. But great that you will be there. Clap very loudly, won't you?"

Donald joined them. "Looks like a little party's going to support you, Jamie."

"Come back after, won't you?"

Tonight was the first real test.

"A tryout," Peter said, when Jamie told him. "It'll become second nature soon. There's still a little of the Scots in your voice – quite attractive, actually."

The theatre was sold out. It went well.

Jamie, to his surprise, didn't think consciously about the new accent, which was a surprise.

In the shared dressing room after, the B-and-B residents piled in through the door. "Hey, you're pretty good, matey," said Willy.

"I think you were wonderful," gushed Clarissa.

"Who would have thought we had a star in our house?" commented Janice.

"Hardly that," Jamie said.

Donald came in behind the group. "Bravo, Jamie, you carried it off fine. Maybe just one little vowel we can look at."

People came, others left. Strangers. Noisy comments. Shaking hands. Until, at last, he was on his own.

Then, as he was removing his makeup, a *"Cooee!"* came from the door. His mother and father stood there, beaming.

"Mum! Dad!"

"Darling! So proud of you. And what have you done with your voice, dear?"

"Good move, Jamie. Well done," said John, smiling.

Donald stood to leave.

"Don't go, Donald; meet my parents." Jamie introduced him. "Donald helped me with my accent."

"That's so kind of you," Linda said. "It's good to find he has a friend."

"My dear, it is my pleasure. I have found a lost youth in helping him. I intend to follow his career with great interest."

Over a drink in his parents' hotel, Linda told Jamie that she was pleased Donald was taking such an interest. "He seems very sensible. An interesting man."

"So, what do you think about my trying to acquire a more English accent?"

"Excellent move. There would be parts you couldn't do, otherwise. Particularly Shakespeare."

"Shakespeare?! I haven't got that far!"

"You never know where you will end up."

"I've a bit to go yet, but I reckon by the end of the run I will have got the hang of it."

Before going to bed, Linda and John talked over Jamie's part in the play, and the new accent.

"It shows commitment."

"He always had that, even as a very young boy; whatever he did, it had to be carried through."

"True. It's still a miracle, though; what could have been a career disaster – you know, the Jeannie affair – has turned out in a way I could never have imagined."

"Neither could I. Am I just being a doting mother when I think he's really good on the stage? He seems to have something you can't learn. A presence. You watch him even when he's not speaking."

"He doesn't know it yet – maybe better that he never does – but it's there, alright."

CHAPTER FOURTEEN

The week passed quickly. The play was well received, with excellent reviews. As each performance came, Jamie found his new accent easier.

Donald came to every performance, the same seat in the same row. After breakfast, he would give Jamie some notes, pointing out certain words that could be improved.

"I will always be pleased I had a hand in it."

"Don't know what I would have done without you, Donald."

"You would have found a way. One thing I have noticed about you, Jamie, is your determination and perseverance. You have a long road ahead. These qualities will be a strong help to you. I just hope I live long enough to see you reach the top of your profession."

"Thanks for your faith in me. It's a great thing, Donald."

"We all need someone. I look on you as a son, my dear – the one I never had."

The week came to an end. The four young ones were leaving.

"'Bye, Jamie. We've all clubbed together and want you to have this." Willy presented a jumper, bearing the motto: *"To Our Good Friend."*

"Gee, that's something! Thank you all. Wish me luck. You all, too."

Donald stayed behind.

"Jamie, good luck, my boy. I have your list of places, and your phone number and email. If I may contact you occasionally, to get your news, that would please an old man."

"And me. Thanks for everything, Donald. Let's contact very soon."

"Jamie, my dear boy, go and find what you are looking for."

CHAPTER FIFTEEN

The next weeks were hectic: arriving at a new town and setting up; performances every evening (two on Saturdays), then off again; sharing cars; laughing; worrying; some good performances, some not so good; some good audiences, some not; learning to milk a laugh; trying not to forget his lines.

He forgot just once, when someone in the front row got up and walked out; for a second, everything left his head. James rescued him, giving him a cue.

"Gee, thanks, James."

"Can happen any time."

The towns included Bristol, then Salisbury, Castle Combe and Marlborough. By now, Jamie had an idea of what touring was all about. He loved it. How right John had been: away from the spotlight was the best training ground. Time to experiment. He felt quite a seasoned actor.

He had been doing some thinking. He had questions, but who to ask? His parents? Yes, they would want to help, but he needed someone with a totally objective view. Peter – would he be the one? Or would he leave himself open to criticism if it got out?

Maybe Mark, but he had a vested interest.

After a lot of struggling with himself, he decided to wait, get the Wilde under way, see how well he could learn a big part.

Back in London, he had just over a week to prepare for rehearsals. He learned quickly. He remembered how he had committed to memory complex medical names without any trouble. "You have a photographic memory," his teacher told him. He read and reread *The Importance of Being Earnest*, imagined the scenes; what he would do, how to say it. By the time rehearsals began he felt fairly confident.

They were rehearsing in the same place as before. How different from his first time there! A beginner, unsure, not even certain he wanted to be there at all.

Not that he was sure yet. Not completely.

Peter called the usual read-through session, then discussions, finally starting to plot the first scenes.

James was the manservant, Lane, doubling as Merriman the Butler, later on. He had a naturally inscrutable face, which he used in the first scene, when Algernon shows what a toff-like fool he is.

It went so well that the rest of the cast ended up in hysterics – a good sign. They had a fortnight to get it up and running, but the play was so funny that sometimes it was difficult not to laugh.

"Get that out of your system, everyone," Peter yelled, after one stop.

By the end of the fortnight they were ready. Timetables and destinations were given out.

This time they were north of the border. One venue was Edinburgh.

"My hometown," he grumbled to James, one evening. "A bit daunting."

"Yeah, can be. My hometown is Cambridge. I know what you mean."

He would not be far from Montrose when the company went to

Carnoustie. He rang his cousin that evening.

"Can we meet up, Alix?"

"That would be terrific, Jamie."

"Lots of news for you. We'll be in Carnoustie in three weeks – in a theatre called The Dibble Tree, would you believe?"

"I know it. Great little theatre. I'll be there, Jamie."

"Just to warn you, I've changed my speaking voice. Had to do it. Och, Alix, so much has happened. It will be great to see you and tell you everything."

"Give me a buzz when you arrive in Carnoustie."

"Will do."

The first date was in Berwick-on-Tweed, just over the border. After that, Dundee, Edinburgh then Carnoustie.

Jamie's first real test was coming. He had a major part, no longer able to hide behind a small role, and he was terrified.

"Listen, Jamie," his father said, when he spoke to his son, realizing that he was having a classic panic attack, "we all go through it. Just say to yourself: 'Do I know it? Deep down, am I confident?' And you have no choice, anyway. I remember my first big role: I nearly crashed out, I was so afraid of failing, but I got there and never did that again."

That steadied Jamie.

The evening came. The first scene. His first line:

"Did you hear what I was playing, Lane?"

"I didn't think it polite to listen, sir."

After that, when the audience had obliged by laughing at all the right places, Jamie settled down. His big scenes were in the first act; after that he had less to do. Gloria was a great Lady Bracknell, and Phyllis a sweet and rather stupid Gwendolyn. Miss Prism was taken by Fanny, who discarded her red talons and scarlet lipstick to play the governess.

After, in the pub, Peter said he was happy. Everyone went to bed pleased.

Next day, the papers were brought in.

"Here's one. My god, he's from Edinburgh! I know him; he can be a sod sometimes."

"Come on, what does he say?" Phyllis cried.

"Read it yourselves, dearie," Bob retorted. "It looks good so far."

Jamie couldn't look. Had he written: *"Jamie Lindsey was badly miscast as the main character,"* or, *"Why did the producer have such a beginner in a major role?"*

"Here's a good bit, Jamie. Come and look," Bob called. He shoved the paper over.

Jamie still couldn't look.

"Go on. It won't eat you."

"Jamie Lindsey, recently a T.V. actor in a popular series, gave an outstanding performance as Algernon. This young actor is a new and exciting face in the younger generation of thespians."

Peter read the reviews. "Well, it looks like we have a winner here, folks. Bravo."

He took Jamie aside. "I was right. Well done. And it can only get better with each performance. You still need to relax a bit but, on the whole, a good performance, Jamie."

"Thanks, Peter. Glad you stuck with me."

Mark rang.

"Seen the papers – great stuff, Jamie. By the way, I've got quite a bit of pay stashing up; when you get back, I'd like to talk about your finding a pad in London. What do you think?"

"If my funds will go that far. I'm back in the middle of next month; I'll give you a ring."

Before leaving the next morning, Jamie rang Donald.

"Good to hear you, Jamie. How's the tour going?"

Jamie read the review to him.

"My, that's just splendid, my boy. I feel a personal triumph for you, knowing the tiny part I played."

The cast set off for Dundee, where they were playing in the Rep Theatre. In two cars they sped up the motorway, passing Edinburgh. The next stop would be back to Edinburgh, before ending the tour in Carnoustie.

Jamie had been to Dundee and he knew the theatre. They were booked into a B-and-B almost next to the theatre. On arrival, they gathered in the theatre, where Peter was waiting for them.

"Hello, everyone. I've had a look inside; they've set up the stage pretty well. So, let's go in and walk around a bit, get used to the slightly different layout."

It was a state-of-the-art theatre: clean dressing rooms, with a small stage and auditorium.

Jamie spent most of the day going over the script, trying to remember where there were weak links, where he could easily forget his lines. He couldn't let up concentration. "That's when you forget the next cue," his father had told him.

Second performance...

Don't think about the critics. Every performance a new one. Jamie remembered what John had said: "Build up stamina."

It went well. He was finding his feet. Getting the feel of playing a role over and over. He could see why touring was a good training ground.

Next stop, Edinburgh.

He rang Linda and John. "Can two of my cast-mates stay in the flat?"

"Of course, Jamie. It will be nice for you all."

"Thanks, Mum. I'm a bit nervous being back here in Edinburgh; it's home territory. Hope the press are kind."

"Always more difficult in your own town. Don't think about it."

Jamie asked James and Bob if they would like to stay in the family flat.

"Thanks, Jamie, that would be terrific."

He arrived at the flat at six p.m. He checked if it was clean and ready, went out, bought food and some drink. The two men arrived soon after.

Between them was a camaraderie that only comes with having been on stage together, having depended on each other to help out in difficult moments, such as line-forgetting – everyone had experienced this. James and Bob were rather laid-back, pleasant men, a bit older than Jamie, and obviously pleased to have landed a good place to stay.

"I'm a pretty good cook, Jamie," Bob told him; "let me do the dinner."

Shortly after, the phone rang. It was Jamie's old headmaster.

"Jamie, I'm going to the performance tomorrow, taking the sixth formers."

"Great, sir! Come back and see me after."

"We're all so delighted at your success."

So, this time it wouldn't be only strangers listening; it would be people who knew him. More difficult, knowing his school was there, the Polish family, old friends he had grown up with… Something bugged him, too: would the press rake up the Jeannie thing?

It was nice to be back in his own bed, though. Beds in B-and-Bs were either lumpy or too small, especially for a man over six feet tall.

That evening, the three young men swanned about the flat, luxuriating in baths, good Scotch and a fine meal, made by Bob.

"This is the life, Jamie," Bob exclaimed.

The theatre was the Lyceum, in Princes Street. The whole cast met in the morning, to check the new set up, walk around a bit.

Peter had some notes to give: "Easy to get sloppy after a few performances; I noticed a few slips at the last performance. So, notes for everyone, please."

John and Linda rang.

"Good luck, darling!" cried Linda. "Give people our love when they come to see you."

Donald rang. "Hope it goes well, my boy; let me know. Wish I was there."

They left for the theatre at five-thirty. This time, Jamie had his own dressing room, his name on the door. He tried to play nonchalant, but it was a bit of a thrill.

Routines had become normal: making up, changing into the period suit, going over text then curtain up. Then over so quickly, cheering from the audience, taking curtain calls. Jamie spotted Aleksi in the front row.

He changed and took his makeup off, just in time to answer knocking at the door. Outside, there was Aleksi, and beside him a lovely girl.

"Jamie, Jamie, so good to see you, dear boy! Remember Olga?"

"Olga?!"

In the three years since Jamie had seen her, Olga had become a lovely woman; tall, auburn hair flowing down her back, huge eyes and a sweet, full-lipped mouth, showing teeth like pearls.

"Gosh, Olga!" was all Jamie could think to say.

"Oh, Jamie, you were wonderful."

"Never stops talking about you," laughed Aleksi.

Behind her stood her husband, a tall, blond, athletic-looking man.

The headmaster arrived with the students: young sixth formers, gazing in awe at Jamie – not so long ago he had been one of them! Smiling, he recognized hero worship.

"That's me, what seems like a lifetime ago."

The headmaster grinned at Jamie. "Impressive, Jamie," he smiled. "And don't forget your promise, to come and speak to my sixth form."

"I haven't forgotten, headmaster. Maybe when the tour is over?"

"I'll keep you to that. And well done; a great play. Everyone did well."

Jamie thought he would never get away: old friends of his parents, some school friends…

He couldn't forget how many of his old friends had shunned him during that horrendous time, when he had been accused of rape. It took some effort to greet them.

Finally, they drifted off.

Then, just as he thought everyone had gone, a knock came at the door. A man stood outside.

"Good evening," he said, with a familiar, lispy Scots voice. Jamie stood transfixed.

"Well, Jamie, that was a great evening. Well done. I believe it's your first big role?"

"Oh, my god," he stammered. "Yes, it is."

"Well done. In your hometown, too, I understand?"

"Yes, that made it even more nerve-wracking. Gosh, I'm glad I didn't know you were there."

The man laughed. "I was curious to see this young actor that everyone is talking about."

"Goodness, surely not."

"You remind me of myself many years ago."

"Gee, thanks, Mr. Connery."

Then he left.

Jamie was stunned, to say the least. "Wow, wait until the others hear."

Bob put his head in. "Come on, Jamie, let's go for a drink."

"Hey, guess who just came to my dressing room!"

The cast gathered in the pub up the street. Edinburgh was quiet at that time of night, the castle looming against the skyline. Jamie loved his town. It was where he had grown up.

I may have an English accent now, but I'll always be a Scot.

"Guess who came to Jamie's dressing room," Bob gushed.

"I know: Oscar Wilde, come back from the dead to say we were stupendous?" suggested Jake.

The answer created a buzz.

"Wow! Going to be the next Bond, Jamie?"

After a few pints, and plenty of adrenalin-driven excitement, Jamie and the two men went back to the flat.

"I think I'll sleep forever," yawned Bob.

"Me, too. Get up when you want tomorrow; we have a day off, between performances. I'm going over to Carnoustie, to see a friend and probably stay the night. You can stay on here; just leave the key where I usually put it."

*

Next morning, he left for Carnoustie. The two men were still sound asleep, their snores filling the flat.

He found a hotel in the same street as the Dibble Tree Theatre. Outside, billboards advertised the play for the following evening. Top of the list of actors was Jamie Lindsey. It wasn't the first time he had seen his name outside a theatre, but he hadn't been in the business long enough to be blasé about it.

As promised, he rang Alix, arranging to meet for lunch. Alix came over when he had finished work.

"Let's hear all about it, Jamie. Things seem to be moving in the right direction okay."

"So far, Alix. First, I want to hear what you are doing."

"I'm in the police force now. Next move, if I pass the exams, is a possible promotion to detective."

"That's great; something you always wanted."

"Guess that business with Jeannie set me off."

"Strange, that, how things worked out for me, too; what was nearly a tragedy ended up in what I'm doing now – the last thing I wanted to do at the time."

"Talking about tragedy, I haven't seen or heard anything about Jeannie for ages. She used to work in a shop, but I heard she was fired, then nothing."

"Guess we can't take on every lost cause. I hope she's okay. Listen, Alix, after the last performance tonight – I've saved a seat for you, by the way – I've decided to go over to Montrose, call on my aunt and uncle – your mother, too – and spend some time with you. After all, I'll be an out-of-work actor soon," he grinned.

"Not for long! Thanks, that's great. I have to say, I am mighty curious to see you acting."

"A warning: I've acquired an English accent, so don't faint."

"Faithless Scot! I suppose it was a good idea. Can you go from one to the other and back again?"

"I've found I can, and I'm not the only one to do that, for guess who came to see me after the performance?"

Jamie told him.

"Cor blimey, now you really are famous!"

Alix went off, leaving Jamie to prepare for the performance. "Getting in the mood," Linda would say.

The Dibble Tree Theatre's name had intrigued him. Carnoustie lay by the Firth of Tay, in Angus; its name came from the Scottish phrase *"craw's nostrie"*, or "crow's nest". A bird's nest in a dibble tree?

"So, what the heck is a dibble tree?"

He looked it up: a tree that grew out of a "dibble" – a garden planting stake. It seemed odd to Jamie; he was no gardener and it meant nothing to him.

Performance time came. At the theatre, before the start, Peter gave them a pep talk:

"Last performance, ladies and gentlemen. Thank you for all your great work on these two tours. I have plans for next year. Let me know if you want to join the group again."

Should he join them again? That was the question he wanted to ask. Had touring been all he wanted?

I need to talk to Mark. What next?

The house was full; a noisy gathering, which died down when the curtain went up.

The character of Lane is setting up the tea, when Algernon enters... and they were off...

Jamie, for the first time, was relaxed, determined to enjoy it. He knew it backward and forward, no longer having to think what came next. His accent flowed.

He came to the section where Jack asks Algernon:

"Any chance of Gwendolyn becoming like her mother in about a hundred and fifty years?"

"All women become like their mothers. That is their tragedy. No man does. That's his."

It got a huge laugh. He could see why comedians love to tell jokes: the laughter; the rush of audience contact. For the first time, Jamie was certain that this was what he wanted to do for the rest of his life. No doubts.

Peter had organized a party afterward; a goodbye get-together.

"Come and join us, Alix."

"I'd better not. But, Jamie, that was fantastic. You are bloody good; I can see that."

"Thanks, Alix. Learning, but enjoying it."

"Give me a buzz when you get to Montrose. Will you stay in a hotel?"

"Yes. I can't stay with Uncle and Aunt, so what's a good place?"

"I know one. I can book, if you want."

"That would be great."

He went off, and Jamie joined the cast in a local café. Everyone was high on adrenalin.

Until this moment, Jamie hadn't realized how much they all meant to him. Friendships formed, every person a link, important to each other. Until it comes to an end.

"Email me, darling."

"Don't forget to ring."

"Write me, love."

But it never happens: other people; other plays; new friends; old ones forgotten…

But he didn't think he would forget them. Francesca the transsexual, a sweet man-become-woman, confused and not happy. Bob, a happy homosexual. Phyllis, one day to be a fine actress; already showing signs. Gloria, a splendid Lady Bracknell, though perhaps not as good as Linda (a bit of bias there).

"Well, ducky," Gloria murmured into Jamie's ear, breathing alcoholic fumes, "such a good-looking man you are; you don't know it yet. Try not to, dearie; nothing worse than a handsome man who looks in the mirror all the time."

"I'll try not to, Gloria."

Speeches. Peter, maudlin after a few drinks, slumped on a chair, while Norman, always the reliable one, got up.

"Let's all thank Peter for his incredible work with us: hip-hip-hurrah!" Everyone joined in.

But there was sadness in the air. Adrenalin was dying down.

Tomorrow, everyone would wake with a headache and a hangover. It did feel like some sort of end to a film which had taken you to a magic world, then it's over and outside it's daylight. Back to the real world.

Jamie said goodnight and goodbye. "Take care, mates. Let's hope we work together again soon."

He was at a plateau. So far, things had gone well. Maybe Mark had ideas. Jamie would ring him.

He wasn't sure why he felt down. After all, there was no need. Probably just mentally tired, he told himself.

After a long sleep, he called Mark.

"Hi, Mark. We've had the last performance, and now I'm wondering what my next move is. Any ideas?"

"Yeah, plenty, but I have some news which might be what you are looking for."

"What?"

"I had a call from a company – a good one – based in London. They are looking for a young Romeo and asked me about you. Would you be willing to audition for the part? Evidently, they saw you in the film."

"Oh, my god, of course! But, when? It's a big one. Have I time to prepare?"

"Rehearsals would begin in October, performances in the new year; you would have several months. First thing, prepare for the audition. There will be plenty of competition."

"Can I do it?"

"It's a big one, Jamie. A make or break."

"I guess."

"I suggest you get down to London. I want to talk to you about having a pad in the city, anyway. Plus, we can go into all the minutiae of what this could do for you. You have only auditioned once, so tips from some actors I know wouldn't be wasted time. Also, if you want to go ahead, a few sessions with an actor who has played the role would be helpful."

"Right, Mark, I'll go to London in five days."

"Ring me when you get here. Cheers, Jamie."

Jamie slept in late the next morning. He felt he had earned it.

Packing up and paying the bill, he got the train to Montrose. As agreed, he phoned Alix.

"I've arrived. Any luck with a hotel?"

"You're booked in. It's in the square, where you and I used to hang around."

"God, yes, I remember."

He walked from the station, booking into the hotel: a typical Scottish building, with its grey stone façade overlooking the busy square.

"Welcome, Mr. Lindsey. May I say how pleased we are to have you with us."

He grinned to himself. How different it would be if I was still that gauche sixteen-year-old hanging around the square, looking at all the girls passing by.

His room was large and sunny: a sitting room with a bedroom off it.

I didn't ask how much this will cost! Jamie wondered. *Oh, to hell with it.*

He relaxed, and ordered some coffee and biscuits. He was hungry; it was some time before meeting up with Alix, and he hadn't had any breakfast.

He had almost dozed off when he heard a knock at the door. Upon opening it, thinking it was the waiter, a woman stood there: small; round-shouldered; bedraggled hair over a face pale and streaked with tears; thin bones jutting out from the rags on her back, which were so dirty that Jamie could smell her from where he stood. She was shivering.

"Can I help you?"

"It's me, Jamie: Jeannie," said a small, tired voice.

"Oh, my god."

"Can I come in, Jamie?"

He let her in, then immediately thought: *I mustn't do this. I'll ring Alix.*

"Alix, can you come over right away?"

"Okay, Jamie. What's the rush?"

"Just get here. You'll see."

He looked at her. She stood there shaking, hands clasped tightly together, knuckles white in distress. Where had Jeannie gone, the provocative, flirtatious, beautiful girl? Surely this person couldn't be her! This pathetic husk of a woman.

"Sit down, Jeannie. Tell me what's happened to you."

She began weeping, shivering so violently her whole body shook. Jamie wondered if she was taking drugs.

A knock came at the door. Jamie opened it to let Alix in.

"What's the hurry?"

"Come in and see."

"Who is that?"

"It's Jeannie."

"What?!"

"I know. I thought you should be here, Alix."

"Dead right I should."

Jeannie sat slumped, tears running down dirty cheeks in rivulets.

"Tell us, Jeannie."

After a few minutes of gulping sobs, she began to speak: "After all that happened in Edinburgh, Mum threw me out. I got a job for a while, then the owner of the shop heard about what had happened and sacked me. I've been living on the streets ever since, part of the nighttime drug world. I guess I went down fast, stealing food where I could, pinching things to feed my habit, selling myself.

"I'm not proud. I never stopped being sorry for what happened – really I didn't, Jamie. Mum wanted to get something out of you."

Alix and Jamie looked at each other.

"Jeannie, go and sit in the bedroom for a minute. Alix and I want to talk."

She went, thin shoulders barely covered by her dirty dress.

"We've got to do something, Alix."

"What, though?"

"She needs to be in some sort of place that deals with drug addicts."

"There is one outside town. Expensive, though. But why should you do this?"

"Because, seeing her like this, I feel guilty. Not my fault what happened, but it all became so sordid and cruel. In the end she was the victim."

"I agree on that. We never did think of her. Why would we?"

"At the time, perhaps not, but seeing her now – a prostitute, a drug user… it's a human tragedy."

"So, what do you think you could do? Or, should I say, we; I'm in it with you."

"Thanks, Alix. All I know is that we can't throw her out, forget she existed."

"It's a bit dodgy, though, Jamie."

"You being a policeman will help. The official line is that here is a girl who needs help."

"Okay, we're in it, so let's get it right."

"Jeannie, come back in."

She fell into the chair, shaking with the need for a fix.

"First of all, go and have a bath, wash your hair. We're going to get some clothes for you while you do that."

"We are?"

"Yes. And, at the same time, Alix, I'll find out about that clinic. Jeannie, you're a size ten, I would think; Alix, buy something: a dress, a jumper… I'll pay you back."

"Right. I hope I can get something Jeannie would like."

"Doesn't matter; just something warm and new."

"Oh, thank you." Jeannie began to weep again.

"Go on, have a bath, make yourself clean."

"I haven't had a bath for months."

She went into the bathroom.

"Think she'll be alright by herself?"

"I can hardly join her! Yes, I would think so. Don't be long, Alix."

"Okay."

Jamie heard Jeannie running a bath. He rang the hotel desk to ask if they knew the name of a rehabilitation clinic outside town.

"Aye, Mr. Lindsey, there's a very good one." They gave him the name. If they were curious, they made no sign; they must have seen Jeannie. Suddenly, he thought: *I hope they don't get the wrong idea!*

"Can you call them for me, please?"

It was ten minutes before the phone rang. It was the clinic. Jamie told them what he wanted.

"That would be no problem. Bring the young woman over and we can assess her."

Just as he put the phone down, Jeannie came out of the bathroom in a towelling dressing gown. "Oh, Jamie, that was wonderful. I don't deserve it. Why are you being so kind?"

"Because of what happened that awful day in Edinburgh. Because you should have had a mother who helped you, instead of destroying you. I was young; I couldn't understand why this was happening, more worried about myself. Someone should have seen what they were doing to you – what we were all doing to you. What's happened to you is terrible, Jeannie; Alix and I want to do something about it. He's getting some clean clothes, then we're taking you to a place where you can be helped."

She sat down, tears falling. "Och, Jamie, I don't deserve you. I tried to ruin your life and now you help me?"

"In a funny sort of way, what happened changed my life; I'm now an actor. So, I have you to thank for that," he smiled.

"You're just being nice, but thanks." She gave him a wan little smile.

"There, you smiled. That's better."

Alix came back with some parcels. "Hope these fit, Jeannie."

She went into the bedroom, coming out with the new clothes on. Alix and Jamie looked at her. With her hair washed and clean clothes on, she began to look a little like the Jeannie they remembered. Just for a moment, the girl had come back, only to vanish again.

"Okay, let's go. Can we use your car, Alix?"

"Yes, sure; I'm off duty today, so no problem."

"Can't believe I'm here with a bobby," Jeannie whispered.

I suppose she wouldn't, Jamie thought; *policemen would be the enemy.*

The clinic lay about five miles outside Montrose. Set in acres of beautiful countryside, the building looked a peaceful place. Inside, Jamie explained what Jeannie needed, and made sure they knew that Alix was a policeman, and that everything was above board.

It was expensive, and for a moment Jamie asked himself why he was doing this. He didn't have to. But this woman, morally bad as she had been, was human, and no one else would help her.

"Get yourself well again, Jeannie," he told her, as she went away. "I'll keep in touch, and Alix will let me know how you are."

In the car back to town, Alix looked at Jamie.

"Och, you're a good man, Jamie. Not many people would have done what you have."

"Couldn't leave her, could we? Turf her out. Yes, she has been a fool but, God, it's an eye opener to see how quickly someone can get into drugs and prostitution."

"Guess you'll be let through the pearly gates."

"I'm no saint. But I'm having my share of luck right now, and the shock of seeing this once beautiful, confident girl reduced to that shaking wretch... well, what else could I do?"

CHAPTER SIXTEEN

Before leaving Montrose, Jamie went to see his aunt and uncle.

"Jamie, dear, it's lovely to see you," his aunt said. "How you've grown, dear."

"Huh, I hear you've joined your mother and father in the acting racket," Uncle said. Time had not mellowed him.

"Yes, Uncle. Finding it a great racket."

"You'll live to regret it. Never did anyone any good, roaming around the country."

"Well, I think it's wonderful," his aunt said. "I won't listen to your uncle."

"Come to something I'm in one day, Auntie."

"Oh, yes, that would be lovely."

"Over my dead body," Uncle lamely retorted, aware he had lost this particular argument.

Jamie saw these two people as he never had before: lonely, cut off from others, his aunt the constant victim of her husband's anger and frustrations.

"I must be off. Lovely to see you both again. Thanks for all the times I stayed with you. It must have been difficult looking after a teenager."

"Not at all, Jamie. I love you very much. Almost like a son you've been."

His uncle said nothing; Jamie would never know what he really thought. Scottish and taciturn as he was, he could and would never reveal any kindness or humanity. *Imagine living with someone like that.*

Even so, he stored how his uncle was for use later, remembering what his father had told him. He saw how his uncle walked: slightly stooped; beady eyes always looking for faults in the world; a moustache bristling with anger at that world. Years later, Jamie would recreate that character on the stage.

He stayed in Montrose until the morning. He and Alix spent the evening together.

"Jamie, I've got something to tell you."

"What's that, Alix?"

"I'm going to get married."

"Hey, that's great."

"I want you to meet her."

"I'd love to. Who is she? In the police force, too?"

"Yes, I met her on a job. In fact, here she is. Morag she's called. I asked her to join us."

A young, strapping girl walked toward them. Not beautiful, but a face full of character and a walk that told the world she was in charge.

"Isn't she something?" her adoring swain murmured.

She marched up to them and sat down, giving Alix a smacking kiss.

"So, you are Jamie? Och, it's great to meet up, at last. If this man of mine ever stops talking about you, I'll be pleased. How do you do?"

"How do you do, too? That's great news."

"Jamie," Alix said, a little shyly, "will you be my best man, laddie?"

"Love to, Alix. When will it be?"

"We plan for September, in our local church, followed by a jamboree in a hall."

These two people seemed to be ideally matched. Alix, a soft-natured man, would have a bride who was strong and capable. They'd make a good team.

They spent the evening together. He told Morag about Jeannie.

"That's an awful story. Tell you what, though: I can keep an eye on her, if you want. Easy just to pop in and see how she's doing. It won't be easy for her if she's been taking drugs."

"Thanks, Morag. That would be terrific."

That was a worry out of the way; Jeannie might just walk out of the clinic. Morag was right: it wasn't going to be easy for her.

He spent the evening with them. Threesomes are never good when two of them are in love. He stayed until eleven, then went to the hotel.

"Give your mother my love, Alix. Apologize that I haven't been to see her."

That night, he fell into bed, exhausted by the emotions of the day. Poor Jeannie. Would she find her way back or was she lost?

He slept late, then left for Edinburgh.

He rang Donald and told him about the Shakespeare.

"Jamie, my boy, that is good news. You will get it; I know you will. But, may I request something?"

"Of course, Donald."

"I have lately been a bit under the weather, and rarely go out anymore; it would give me tremendous pleasure if you could find the time to visit this old man."

"I would love to. I have to go to London tomorrow, to talk to my agent, but I could come to you next week, if that would suit you."

"That would be fine, Jamie. I will email you my address and a map to find my place."

He then rang his old headmaster.

"Keeping my promise, sir: happy to talk to your students. Give me a date that would suit. I'm up here in September for a wedding, so maybe around then. Will term have started?"

"Good news. I'll be in touch with suggestions."

CHAPTER SEVENTEEN

Before leaving for London, Jamie phoned his parents, to tell them about the possible audition and to get their feelings. It was a huge step; he wanted to know if he was going too fast, too soon. John knew how important it was to get this right.

"No, I don't think so; worth a try. Romeo is a young role; many great actors started with it. I believe Gielgud played it early on, in his twenties."

"Can I learn it in time? Assuming I get it."

"Yes, I think so. It would need total concentration and commitment."

Linda took the phone. "Darling boy, a perfect Romeo you would be."

He told them what Mark had said.

"That's a good idea: getting someone who has played the part."

It looked as though he was committed. It excited him and challenged him, yet he had that fear of the unknown, something he'd had before nearly every performance: fear of failure. He once read that Laurence Olivier always had stage fright, and he could believe it.

Would he have gone into acting if he had known how frightening it could be at times? That the challenges he faced were unknown factors. In medicine, he would have known what was coming; in this profession, he never did. If he was honest, deep down he enjoyed that.

"Guess it's in my blood."

Before getting the train to London, he dug out his parents' copy of

Romeo and Juliet. Might as well start; see what he had to take on.

CHAPTER EIGHTEEN

He rang Michael and Mary when he got to London.

"Of course you can stay, Jamie. Longing to get your news."

"I've really come to see Mark, to discuss some things with him."

"Ask him over for a meal, then you can be comfortable together."

He rang Mark.

"Yeah, great, Jamie; nice people. I'll be over around six. Lots to talk about."

He had read through *Romeo and Juliet* on the train; could he learn all that?! Pages of speeches? He was surprised at how many he recognized, until he remembered he had covered it for his exams at school. But could he learn such a big role? Was he ready for it, or was he always going to have doubts, for every new challenge?

Mark arrived on the dot – a small, dark-skinned, wiry man, every fibre of his slim frame exuding energy. Even his hair, black and curly, seemed to crackle with his enthusiasm.

"Hi, Jamie. Well, you've put on some meat since we last met – looks good; more mature, in a way. So, how was Edinburgh? Did the tour go well?"

"I think it did. We got some good reviews. All the actors in the group were pretty nice to work with. I will say I had a good initiation into acting, as you and my parents said I would."

"Good, I thought it a good idea. I have heard back from Peter: he was pleased; very encouraging, what he said."

"A great guy to work with. I guess maybe I've been lucky."

Mary served the meal.

"Am I right? You're thinking of a place in London?"

"It's an idea. London is central. All depends maybe on whether he gets this part."

"Well, in that case, a flat has just come on the market across the road, in that block you can see from here."

"Probably too expensive, Mary."

"I can find out, if you want."

Mark interrupted: "That's something I want to talk about, Jamie. The film you made is coughing up some nice repeat fees – it seems to have been a success – so you have some finances building up, plus your pay from the tour."

"Maybe give me some idea how much I could budget for. As for the film, will you believe that I've never seen it, except when we saw the first rushes. Everything moved so fast I forgot about it."

"Well, I've recorded it," Mary laughed, "so we will make up for that tonight."

"Oh, God, am I ready for this?"

After supper, they both went into the bedroom to talk.

"I've told the company that you would like to audition for Romeo. They will send me audition times. I would suggest an early slot, before they get tired."

"What should I prepare?"

"Choose a section where Romeo has some meaty speeches, lasting about five to ten minutes."

"I've had a look, and I think I've picked out something suitable."

"Great, you and I are going to work well together. You are getting some good exposure already; it's going round a bit. The acting game is full of gossip – people talk to each other – and occasionally I've heard you mentioned."

"That's scary."

When they returned to the lounge, Mary had the film ready to show. Jamie hadn't seen himself since the initial viewing. Was that him: muscular, tanned; a young man, sleeves rolled up over tanned arms, blue eyes looking into the camera? It was a weird experience. He could see that he did a fairly decent job; in fact, the scene with the mother came over well.

"Hmm, quite a heartthrob," Mary grinned.

"Go on! I can't see that."

"Yes, really. The camera likes you."

"Someone else said that. I suppose it's a good thing."

"If film is what you will do later, a very good thing."

Mark left soon after the film was over. "I'll let you have those dates, Jamie. Speak soon."

Next morning, Mary had made some calls about the flat across the road.

"It's very small: just one-bedroom, a tiny lounge, kitchen and bathroom. Might not be too expensive. Shall I find out?"

"No harm in asking. Doubt if I'm well off enough to buy it, though."

"Let's see. It would be ideal. We could keep an eye on it for you."

She rang the estate agent.

"Yes, it is on the market. Needs a lot done to it, though. Very tiny; only suitable for one person."

The price was not too bad – understandably, as it was at the top of the building, with no lift, needing a lot of T.L.C.

"Try to get the price down," Michael said.

Would he get a mortgage? He was only nineteen and an actor; actors are always expected to be unreliable, and often out of work.

"I think your work to date might impress a mortgage company. Mark could back you up."

Jamie rang Mark on his mobile. He was on the tube, so hearing him was difficult.

"Depends on what you pay for it. Let me know and we'll go from there."

"Let's put in a crazy offer. What's to lose?" Michael suggested.

Jamie rang the agent and offered £65,000 under the asking price.

"They'll never accept that."

CHAPTER NINETEEN

They did. Now he had to find out if he could get a mortgage. In the meantime, they went to see the flat. It was at the very top of the building; pour flights of stairs.

"Phew," puffed Jamie, after they had toiled up. "Suppose it will do as a first buy."

"You'll be on the property ladder. That's important," said practical Michael.

Mary looked out of the window. "It's actually quite nice; a great view over the houses, and it would shape up nicely with some coats of paint and furniture."

Mark rang.

"I hear you've already found somewhere."

"Just been to see it: very small. Just right for now, though, Mark. Point is they've accepted sixty-five thousand less. Am I mad to commit?"

"Get a mortgage; we can manage a down payment, and then I can assume your earnings will take care of it."

"Property owner – that sounds good."

"Gives you a base. Good move, Jamie."

Next day, he went to see the mortgage people. If they wouldn't cough up, then he couldn't do it.

"We see you have been on the television – in fact, I and my wife enjoyed it – and you have just completed a tour in Scotland. It would seem, Mr. Lindsey, that you are going places, and it would be in our interest to offer you a mortgage on this property," said Mr. Smith, at the mortgage company.

"Thank you." He was off! At nineteen, he was a property owner!

"We'll help you get it up and running," Mary suggested. "Stay with us until it's completed and ready to move into."

"I've promised to go and see a friend so, when I get back, I'll go and buy things to start getting it ship-shape. I'll have to get a bed, some furniture and kitchen stuff."

Mary chipped in: "I'll look around some junkyards and second-hand shops; we have plenty round here."

"She'll have a ball; probably have lots of things on the go when you get back."

Next day, Jamie set off for Rickmansworth, where Donald lived. Getting off the train, he asked for directions; did they know Donald Carstairs?

"Oh, Sir Donald? Yes, indeed." They gave directions. "Would you like a taxi?"

"Sir Donald?!" He'd never said a word about that.

Jamie rang him.

"Jamie! Come along, my boy, get a taxi. I'm about three miles down the road, up a long drive."

It was a very long driveway, winding until a big, Georgian-style house came into sight. Donald was waiting for him at the door.

"This is wonderful, Jamie. Welcome to my home. Come in, my boy. We can talk over lunch."

Lunch was served by a stout, middle-aged woman, obviously devoted to Donald.

Inside, the house was elegant: furniture from the Georgian era; curtains in subtle silks and brocades.

"My wife's tastes. She was an interior designer."

"It's lovely."

"Now, Jamie, tell me what's been happening. I know about the Shakespeare. Will that come about?"

"Only if I get chosen. I'll audition next month. Meantime, I have to get working on an audition piece."

"You've come a long way from the insecure young man I first met."

"Guess I have. And I'm curious, Donald: why were you in that B-and-B, rather than a nice hotel? It was hardly a great place for you."

"I wanted to mix with ordinary people, experience a side of life that I had never really seen. Cocooned at the gallery, I never seemed to mix with anyone but rather stuffy art people. So, I put a pin on a hotel map in Bath and landed there."

"Glad you did; that was my luck."

"It was fun, wasn't it? I'll always look upon it as one of my nicest experiences, Jamie."

Over the next two days, they forged a close relationship. They had much in common, and Donald, in his wisdom, opened up many avenues.

"Don't be tunnel-visioned. Keep learning. Look at art and music. Let a knowledge of history in the arts, in mankind, enrich your work as an actor."

To a nineteen-year-old, the wisdom of this man would stay with Jamie all his life.

Soon the time came when he had to go.

"Come any time, Jamie," Sir Donald said, as Jamie left in a taxi.

He was not to know that he would never see this wonderful man again.

CHAPTER TWENTY

Back in London, he got the tube over to Mary and Michael.

Mary looked happy. "I've found some things for you."

"Been having a ball," teased Michael.

"Thanks, Mary. What have you found?"

"There was a double bed for sale in the *Friday Ad*, so I went to see it. Would be perfect. Hardly used, as the owner went abroad and his son wanted to get rid of it. I put a deposit down, hoping that would be okay."

"Gosh, thanks. What do I do now?"

"Ring the son, say you want it. Will he send it to the address? Offer to pay for the service."

"The address? It isn't mine yet."

"The vendor is happy to let us furnish it before completion. If it falls through, we'll just go and get it."

"Falls through?" Jamie gulped.

"You're getting a lesson in ordinary, basic things, Jamie," Michael grinned.

"Well, thanks, Mary. I'll get on with it."

"Listen, Jamie, I know you have to get the audition ready; I suggest you put time aside for that, then gradually get the flat ready."

"That's what I thought I would do."

"Don't let her boss you, Jamie. She tends to take over."

"Thanks for that, partner. From now on I shall not help."

"Only joking, sweetie. You are my tower of strength."

She was right: Jamie knew he needed to get down to work.

That night he lay in bed with the play in front of him. He had chosen the famous speech: *"But soft! What light through yonder window breaks?"* Now he had to learn it; decide how to play it. He found the Shakespearian couplets easy to get his tongue around. He had read somewhere that it had, for modern ears, to roll easily, as if it was natural to speak in rhymed verses.

He wanted this part. In his bones, he felt he could do it. The very thought made his heart go a little faster. Somewhere, long ago, he had stood with Shakespeare; in his genes were generations of actors, going back to Elizabethan times. No wonder his parents had hoped he would continue that line – only to find their son wanted to be a doctor. He understood them better now.

Gradually, he committed the lines into his head, then declaimed, into the mirror.

"I heard you last night, Jamie. How is it going?"

"Okay, I think. I've almost learned the passage. It's how to put it over."

"Try it on us, then. Use us as sounding boards."

"Hey, that would be helpful. But be critical; pull me to bits."

"That's a deal. Right after dinner, session one."

Now the first test.

He felt it went well. Just a few fluffs.

"If I might suggest something," Mary said, after hearing it through, "have you thought yet about who you are? What the situation is with you and Juliet? You know, the political aspect; that this love is fatal, even if neither of them realize it yet. Getting inside the skin of the part. This young man is madly in love, yet it is destructive. How love and overwhelming passion can blind you to reality?"

"Gosh, Mary," Michael grinned, "profound stuff."

"Let me think about it, then try again."

"Have a glass of wine to loosen you up," Michael suggested.

It did. He began again.

Then, something happened: he forgot Mary and Michael. Shakespeare's words were flowing, ending with: *"O, that I were a glove upon that hand, that I might touch that cheek!"*

A silence fell.

"Well, Jamie, I think you've found the key. That was much better."

"It felt easier, but I'll work on it. That was helpful. Thanks, both of you."

That night, as they lay in bed, Mary commented: "You know what? I think Jamie is going to be a great actor. Did you see how he completely forgot about us?"

"I did. And I agree; he has something rare."

"And we were there at the beginning."

"Maybe it's your cooking."

"Oh, ha, very funny. But I do think, if he can impress the audition people, he'll be on his way."

Jamie couldn't guess what they were saying in the next room, but he had begun to realize that he had in him something he couldn't understand. And that he shouldn't try to.

Next day, Mark emailed over the audition times; Jamie had three weeks before they took place. He chose a slot on the fourth day, at eleven-thirty in the morning.

"That's good, Jamie," Mark emailed back: "gives them time to hear lots of others, and at eleven-thirty they are still not tired or too hungry."

An email then came from Alix:

"Wedding 4th September, Jamie. Still ok for you? Hope so. Must have you as my best man."

"It's on. Book me that same hotel. I'll be up the night before. Are you having a stag night?"

"Aye, of course."

"See you then."

CHAPTER TWENTY-ONE

On September 3rd he travelled back to Scotland, calling in at Edinburgh to collect his kilt and various extras. The Lindsey tartan was made up of maroon, green and navy blue. He had a velvet jacket, lace shirt, stockings and his dirk: an elegant, jewelled one given to him on his eighteenth birthday, by an aunt.

In Montrose, he went to the hotel then rang Alix.

"I'm here, Alix; let me know where the stag do is. And have you news of Jeannie?"

"I'll pick you up at seven. And, yes, Jeannie's had her problems. Morag called to see her nearly every day; I think without that she would have scarpered."

"I was afraid of that. So, what's happened?"

"That's a surprise. Wait and see."

Alix arrived at seven, dressed in his Robertson tartan, made up of blues and greens, with a red line running through.

"Och, man, are ye not in your tartan?"

"Tomorrow, Alix; I've brought it."

"Well, let's go and celebrate my last day of freedom."

"I think Morag will be worth the sacrifice," Jamie laughed.

"Aye, she's a wonderful woman."

The stag do was in a pub. Between his friends from school and police friends – big, strapping lads – it was a noisy, rather raucous crowd. Alix knew how to enjoy himself, downing copious amounts of beer and ending up singing Scottish songs.

"Robbie Burns lyrics, Jamie. Now, there's a man who knew how to enjoy himself."

"And the ladies."

"Ah, but he never knew Morag; he wouldn't have looked at another woman if he had."

What could you say after that?

Everyone ended up slightly, if not copiously, drunk. Jamie rolled back to his hotel, to fall into bed.

Alix's last words were: "I'll come for you at eleven tomorrow. Don't sleep in. Night, Jamie." Then he staggered off home.

Jamie woke at nine, had breakfast downstairs then dressed. He wasn't aware of it, but the dress kilt with the shirt, velvet jacket and stockings had turned him from a good-looking young man into a stunning one. Tartan, lace and velvet could transform even the ugliest man into a swan.

Alix arrived to pick him up.

"I have the ring. Keep it safe, Jamie. It's a great day for me, laddie."

"Yes, Alix. And don't worry; I'll do you proud."

"Of course you will, my best friend."

The wedding was in a small church outside St. Cyrus; a simple ceremony. Jamie didn't drop the ring, and it went off without a hitch. Coming out, Alix's fellow policemen formed a line down which the newly married couple walked, Morag in a white, simple dress, auburn hair tied back with flowers.

Afterward, everyone gathered in a small hall in St. Cyrus, overlooking the sea, where through a window you could see the ocean, the sun shining on the waves as they crashed on the rocks. Lunch was served by a couple of girls.

As Jamie sat talking, a voice behind him said: "Hello, Jamie."

Turning, he saw a girl stood there. Blonde. Slim. Smiling.

"Aye, it's me."

It was Jeannie.

Jamie got up. "Jeannie!"

"A surprise. I hoped you could come: I wanted you to see that I managed. And to thank you. I'm much better; I've got a flat, a job, and it's all because of you."

"There, I knew you'd do it. Clever girl."

"Might not have done; I hated it at the clinic. But Morag came; that helped a lot."

Alix joined them. "Nice surprise, Jamie?"

"I'll say. Keep it up, Jeannie."

"Aye, I will."

Time for speeches. Jamie had put something together: their friendship, etc. Some jokes made everyone laugh. They were so young; at nineteen, Jamie didn't feel that marriage was for him yet. And he hadn't met anyone, anyway.

He stayed until the next morning.

"See you soon, Alix. By the way, where are you going for your honeymoon?"

"Up to the Highlands. We both love walking and exploring."

"By the way, tell Morag thanks for Jeannie; she told me how it helped. Do you think she can stay the course?"

"God knows; it's up to her now. Morag will still look in on her, but it depends on how far she went with drugs; you know what they say: it's difficult to kick."

"Well, we did our bit. Seeing her yesterday was a surprise. At least we didn't waste our time."

"I'll keep you posted. Good luck with the audition. Let me know."

Before he left, he paid the bill for the clinic. It took a chunk out of his bank balance. Would Jeannie stick to her new life? Had she given up throwing herself at men?

I'll probably never know.

CHAPTER TWENTY-TWO

He had promised his old headmaster he would speak to his students.

"What on Earth can I say? I'm not much older than they are; they might think it a cheek."

"That's the reason I asked you, Jamie," the headmaster said: "they will relate to you better than some old person who has forgotten what it's like to be young. Don't forget, for a student of fourteen, even nineteen seems old."

He put some notes together, then made his way over to his old school.

The school hall was packed. Looking at the faces, he wondered how he would have felt about someone like him arriving to tell them how great they were, which he wasn't going to do. *Remember,* he told himself, *youth judges without mercy.* But what could he say that could stir them? What angle would get to them?

"Well, hi, everyone. I'm going to surprise you today. Why? Because I remember that once I sat where you're sitting today, and not that long ago, listening to a man who, as far as I could see, was, to my fourteen-year-old eyes, well past his sell-by date. Of course, he wasn't, but I remember my feeling: *Who is this old git? What's in it for me?*" (Laughter.) "Well, there was a lot, but I didn't know it then.

"Recently, I met an eighty-year-old man who has become my best friend. Wise, with a lived life, he looked at this young man and opened doors for me that will never shut again."

He talked for an hour, getting involved in what he was saying. The children didn't interrupt once; there was just silence.

"So, all I can say," he ended, "is we try to become wiser, but it takes time. So, find your own eighty-year-old and let him open your eyes."

He was given three cheers and the students clustered around him.

"Phew, Headmaster, that was worse than a performance."

"Got it just right, Jamie."

CHAPTER TWENTY-THREE

He caught the night train to London, arriving at Mary and Michael's in time for breakfast.

"We want to hear all your news: the wedding, the school talk and Jeannie; how was she? Had she run away?"

"She's okay; turned up as a waitress at Alix's wedding shindig. I think she'll be alright."

"Right, now, Jamie, work."

"Yes, Mary."

"Watch out, she'll beat you."

"Oh, Michael, stop that. It's only for his own good. How are you getting on with Romeo? And what about Juliet; I wonder who will get the part."

"I thought about that. I'm going to suggest Phyllis Johns; she was on the tour and very ambitious. She played Gwendolyn."

He rang Mark.

"I do know of her. Is she feminine and very good-looking?"

"Extremely. Big potential, I think."

"Okay, I'll look into it."

The mortgage for the flat had come in and the double bed arrived. Jamie and Mary looked around some second-hand shops, and they found a junkyard which had old pine going for a song – there they found a table, chairs and an old sofa. "Just needs a re-cover."

The flat's floor was pine. "Give it a shine and all you need are a few mats or small rugs."

*

While Jamie worked on the audition, the flat purchase completed surprisingly quickly. Within a few weeks he was ready to move in.

"Let's have a launch party," Mary suggested, "get a few friends in, maybe Mum and Dad."

So, one evening a crowd of people squeezed into Jamie's new abode. Linda and John came down, as well as Mark, his girlfriend, Ann, and Phyllis Johns.

"Jamie, I've just heard about the auditions. Thank you so much."

"Be fun if we both get it."

"Wouldn't it? All depending, maybe we could work on it together."

"Good idea."

Phyllis was a petite girl in her early twenties. Soft, blonde hair framing an angelic face. Big, blue eyes looked out on the world with an innocent, attractive gaze.

"I guess this is the chance I've been looking for."

"Could be. New territory for me; I've only auditioned once."

"I've done dozens. Hate them, actually, but we have to do it."

"Where are you based?"

"With my parents, in Willesden. They have a flat, and so far I've not been able to move away. This flat's great, Jamie."

"If you don't mind the climb."

Linda and John arrived, breathless after climbing the stairs.

"Jamie, this is super!" cried Linda.

"Good move," his father added, a bit out of breath.

"Linda! John!" Mark embraced them. "This son of yours is doing okay."

"This Romeo part would be something."

"Don't make too much of it, Dad; I'm nervous enough already."

"Remember what I've said: preparation – that helps the nerves."

Jamie brought Phyllis over. "Phyllis is auditioning, as well."

"Wasn't your mother an actress?" Linda queried.

"Yes, she was, under the name of Margaret Williams."

"I was in a play with her – oh, gosh, years ago. I remember her well," cried Linda.

"She has mentioned you ever since I was on tour with Jamie."

"Give me her telephone number. I'll ring her."

John and Linda didn't stay long. "We have to get back; we just wanted to see you and this flat. We're glad you've got a base, and that Mary and Michael are just across the road; I won't worry so much about you."

"Well, she will, but not as much," grinned John.

"Phyllis is nice, isn't she, John?" Linda said, as they made their way to King's Cross.

"Now, don't match-make."

"No harm in thinking it. Jamie hasn't had a proper girlfriend; maybe it's time."

"You know what? I think that Jeannie affair put him off."

"I've wondered about that. It says something about our son that he can go and help her, after what she tried to do to him!"

"It does. I'm proud of him."

With only ten days to go before the audition, Jamie spent some of it getting his flat habitable. Mary popped up quite a lot, finding kitchen things for him she didn't need. They went out and got a microwave oven, then a fridge. The men who delivered were not too happy with the stairs.

"Cor blimey," one of them gasped, "need to be young to do this."

Jamie spoke to Phyllis a few times. She'd had her audition on the second day.

"How did it go?"

"Can't tell. They didn't do the 'we'll call you; don't call us' routine, anyway."

"I'm on tomorrow. Wish me luck."

"Let me know, Jamie."

He got to the theatre in good time. Having thought how best to prepare, he sat out of sight, getting into the mood; who he was: Romeo. Why he was there: to see Juliet. A man full of passion, blindly in love.

At eleven, he was called. Walking onto the stage, the usual panic hit him, lights blinding him. Everything left his head. He couldn't remember the first line.

He heard his father's voice: "Relax, Jamie. Go for it, boy."

He began:

"But soft! What light through yonder window breaks?"

And he was off.

He forgot the people sitting in darkness below him in the theatre, the crew watching; all that mattered was the moment, and that he loved Juliet.

"O, that I were a glove on that hand, that I might touch that cheek!"

For a moment, nobody said anything. Jamie stood there, still part of the emotions that had filled him.

"Thank you, Jamie. We'll be in touch."

He hadn't a clue about how it had gone. He had his usual negative thoughts: *Why should I get it? There were seasoned actors there. Oh, well, put it down to experience; did the best I could do. Shouldn't listen to friends and family; they're biased. Not too late to go back to being a doctor.*

"Now, stop that, Jamie!" Mary said, when he had supper with them. "Just wait and see."

He was getting that awful thing that actors get: the let-down. When every fibre of his being was leading up to that moment, but now it was over; a plunge into despair. He couldn't sleep; if he dozed off, he dreamed he was out on a stage, with voices calling:

"Why have you bothered?"

"I don't know."

Waking to face another day of waiting was like facing the guillotine.

Two days after the audition, Mark rang.

"Well, Jamie, I've got news."

His heart stopped for a second. *Here it comes.* They didn't want him.

"You've got it."

"What do you mean?"

"They want you to play Romeo."

He couldn't answer.

"Jamie, did you hear? You've got the part."

"Gee, Mark, I was so sure I hadn't."

"And Phyllis has got Juliet."

Ringing off, he told Mary and Michael, who were in the kitchen.

"I knew it! I knew it!" Mary cried, dancing around in her excitement. "Now you and Phyllis can get together and work on it. Couldn't be more perfect!"

Phyllis rang an hour later.

"We've done it, Jamie! Now I'm scared out of my wits!"

"Haven't had time yet to think. Let's meet up, plan our strategy."

"First thing: learn the part. Second: work toward how we do our roles."

"A challenge."

When Linda and John heard, they were in a mixture of euphoria and fear for Jamie.

"It's such a big thing to take on, John!"

"Yes, but it seems our son has developed into someone who takes a challenge."

"If he should do a good job, you do realize that his career is made, Linda?"

"Guess you're right. Who could have guessed?"

The theatre rang the next morning.

"Can you come and see us, Jamie? Discuss things?"

"Sure. Say when."

"Make it next week. Phyllis Johns is coming, too. We are pleased to have found you both. What we want to do is give you our plans, let you know how long you have to learn the role, then begin rehearsals. Your agent has been in touch; fees are agreed, plus some expenses, all of which I hope is fine with you. We know you have to live, and don't want you to worry about money."

"Thanks."

"There will be a get-together with the rest of the cast fairly soon."

Jamie knew what this meant. He had been given a chance to make something of himself as an actor. If he still felt that everything had happened too fast, he also felt, deep down, that he could do it.

He got the Shakespeare book out again, looking at it. Now it was the whole play he had to learn; great, long passages. He'd start straight away, go to bed with it.

Don't they say putting it under your pillow helps it to stick? Might try that.

Phyllis rang.

"How shall we work together?"

"We have four months, so I understand from Mark. How about, the first month learn as much as we can, then get together to run it through?"

"You know, Jamie, it's great that we knew each other."

"It is, isn't it; I was thinking that, too. A strange Juliet might have been trickier. Imagine my not liking her!"

"Well, I like you – very much."

"Ditto."

And he did. He had been very aware of her on tour. She had a warm personality and she was intelligent. And now he was going to have as close a contact as two young people could have: lovers on stage.

CHAPTER TWENTY-FOUR

The following week he was called to the theatre. It was the first time he had seen the directors; at the audition they had sat behind lights, just dark, invisible figures. Upon getting there, the first person to greet him was the producer, John.

"Hi, Jamie. I'm John Hopkins. Great to meet you, and congrats on getting the role."

"Thanks, John. I'm really looking forward to it."

"We've been lucky to find you and Phyllis: you're young, not yet very well known, and as Romeo and Juliet your youth is perfect. Plus, you're both bloody good."

He was joined by another man.

"Jamie Lindsey, great to meet you. I'm the fencing master. We'll be working together."

Fencing? Jamie hadn't thought about that.

The door opened and Phyllis came in. Introductions again.

"Okay, folks, here's our programme: launch in February next year; start rehearsals proper at Christmas, leaving you both some time to learn your roles. You'll be called in occasionally to talk over progress. We open at the Globe Theatre, by the way."

"Oh, my god! I didn't realize that!" Jamie gasped.

John smiled. "I thought I'd surprise you. Let me tell you, it will be an experience you'll never forget. The theatre is an extraordinary place."

The meeting went well and Jamie felt reassured. Phyllis was also pleased.

"This is going to be special, Jamie," she whispered as they left.

"Sure is. Come on, let's go and celebrate. Do you like seafood?"

"Love it."

"Right, the oyster bar in Covent Garden. Let's get a taxi."

"We could get the tube."

"Not today. Let's make it a day to remember, Phyllis."

The oyster bar was pretty full, but the waiter found a table.

"Your first time, sir?"

"Yes, actually."

"Ah, good." He went away wreathed in smiles.

"I like it here," Phyllis pronounced: "good atmosphere, great smells…"

The waiter came over. "Sir, wine for you and the lady?"

Jamie hadn't done much wine choosing, but he had seen his father ordering.

"Yes, the Sauvignon Blanc would be fine."

"Excellent choice."

"Jamie, that was clever; I wouldn't know one wine from another."

"Neither do I. A guess."

They dined on shellfish – oysters and clams – washed down with the white wine. Phyllis was good to talk with. Watching her as she smiled and answered a question, Jamie was attracted to her. With her elfin face framed by honey-gold hair, a low, musical voice and sense of humour, he was entranced.

"How old are you, Phyllis, if you don't mind my asking?"

"Of course not, Jamie. I'm twenty… and a bit."

"I'll be twenty in a couple of weeks. I guess we are the right age for the play. Even a bit old," he laughed. "After all, isn't Juliet only sixteen?"

"I think she is. And Romeo not more than seventeen."

"My god, we're a couple of geriatrics," he laughed.

Asking for the bill, Phyllis insisted on making it Dutch.

"Not tonight; it's my treat. I wanted to do something we might never forget."

"Well, you have, Jamie. Guess it's a day we'll both never forget."

CHAPTER TWENTY-FIVE

For the next month, Jamie worked, pressing words into his memory bank. John had found a sword master, and once a week he went to the teacher's studio.

"You can't be an expert in just a few weeks," the teacher told him, "but you are getting some idea. Practise is the only way to go."

He met up with an actor who had played Romeo many years before.

"Possibly my favourite role. I was young, energetic and the words are so wonderful. If I can give you any help, Jamie, I would be pleased."

"Am I getting the flow of the Shakespeare right? That would be a help."

"Let's hear what you're doing with it."

For the next few weeks, he put Jamie through exercises and criticized. "But in the end, Jamie, that's all I need to do. You have a natural affinity with this text; I don't want to disturb that. So, good luck. I'll be there to cheer you on."

He was over at Mary and Michael's place most days, Mary insisting he had his meals with them. "Save you cooking."

One morning, a letter arrived – a formal-looking envelope, with a lawyer's name on the back. Opening it, Jamie read:

"*We are sorry to advise you that Sir Donald Carstairs has died. It is in your interest to call and see us, as there is a matter to discuss.*'

"Oh, my god!" Jamie groaned. "He can't have."

"Jamie, what is it?" Mary cried.

"That wonderful old man I met in Bath. He's died."

"Oh, my dear, I'm so sorry." Mary came over and put her arms around him.

"I had no idea that I would never see him again."

He went to bed with a heavy heart. Sir Donald had become a dear friend, who had wanted to be there when Jamie succeeded. So much a part of those Bath days. Suddenly, he was gone. Jamie was not ashamed to weep that night.

The next morning, Mary asked him what he wanted to do.

"The letter says I should go and see Donald's lawyer. I can't imagine what for."

"Maybe Sir Donald has left you a little something."

"I'll ring them."

"Ah, yes, Mr. Lindsey. So sad; such a fine man. Can you call in over the next few days; there is a matter to discuss."

"Yes, when would suit you?"

"Tomorrow, perhaps?"

"I could manage that."

"Shall we say eleven-thirty?"

"Fine, I'll be there."

The office was in Rickmansworth High Street. Going in, Jamie was met by an efficient-looking, elderly woman at an impressive desk.

"Ah, yes, Mr. Lindsey. I'll call Mr. Jones."

Mr. Jones came down, a small, overweight man, whiskers resplendent around a little nose, on which half-moon glasses resided.

His main feature was the largest eyebrows Jamie had ever seen, bristling with animation.

"Mr. Lindsey, would you please come into my office?"

His was a warm-looking, welcoming room, with red curtains and walls. A large antique desk bristled with papers and numerous photos of, Jamie assumed, Mr. Jones's family.

"Mr. Lindsey, I gather from what Sir Donald told me that he had acquired a great affection for you. He gave me some idea of how you and he met, which I must say was very interesting."

"Thank you."

"However, in the last few weeks, as Sir Donald felt his time was ending, he came to me to make a new will. He had no family left, and therefore no descendants that he could leave his estate to. So, it is with great pleasure that I can tell you Sir Donald has left his entire estate to you."

"What?! Surely not!"

"Yes, indeed. If I may, I will read you his will." He opened a document on the desk.

"*'I leave my whole estate to Jamie Lindsey, who made my life so interesting in my last days, and for whom I developed much affection. However, as this young man is on the cusp of success, and would not perhaps benefit from great amounts at this time, I leave him the sum of twenty-thousand pounds to help him at this point in his career; the rest of my estate I put into a trust, to be opened when Jamie is thirty. If, however, Jamie should need any emergency finances, I leave that open to the discretion of my lawyers.'*"

"There you have it, Mr. Lindsey."

"I really don't know what to say! That Sir Donald has done this is something I wouldn't have dreamed of. I didn't even know he was a knight until long after I had met him."

"He was a very modest man. I understood from Sir Donald that he had tremendous faith that you are going to be a fine and successful actor. He wanted to help."

"He was a wonderful man."

"So, now all I have to do is draw you a cheque or bank transfer, whichever you prefer. From now on I will occasionally contact you. And, if you want any more funds, as it says in the will, contact me. By the way, Sir Donald also left a large legacy to the Tate Gallery."

"He loved it there."

Jamie left. Had he dreamt all this? What had he done to deserve it? He'd had such a short time with Donald, yet their friendship, separated by nearly sixty years in time, had become deep and long-lasting. Did the old man want Jamie's dreams to come true? Jamie knew he did. And, goodness, wouldn't that money make a difference. Now he could work on the play without any money worries.

"One day I'll remember Donald in some way. That I promise myself."

CHAPTER TWENTY-SIX

Back with Mary and Michael, and Mary was bursting with curiosity. "What happened, Jamie?"

"Something incredible."

"Tell me. I'm dying to know."

He told them. "…And his estate is in a trust until I'm thirty."

Mary flopped down on the sofa. "Oh, my god, Jamie, that is one of the most heart-warming and wonderful things I've heard. What a friend you made. And what a difference this will make."

"And sensible of your friend to put the main estate in a trust," Michael commented.

"You know that old saying, about being hungry to succeed."

"Knowing his thinking, you're probably right."

"No money worries now."

"Guess so."

That evening, he told his parents.

"You know, Jamie," his father said, when he heard, "sometimes I wonder if you have a guardian angel looking out for you."

"Whatever it is."

"You gave something special to Sir Donald when he most needed it."

"One day, I'll do something so he is remembered. He'd like that."

"What he would want is to see you up there on a stage, becoming a great actor," Linda said. "I didn't know him but, from what you've told us, he loved what you were striving for."

"Probably right, Ma. By the way, guess where the play will take place."

"The Haymarket? The Old Vic?"

"The Globe Theatre."

"Oh, my god!" Linda exclaimed. "That's fantastic."

"Come whole circle," John commented; "one of our ancestors acted in the original Globe. Not with Shakespeare, however; he never set foot in it."

"Is it covered? What if it rains?"

John laughed. "It is covered. The only uncovered bit is the main section."

"Well, Ma and Pa, from now on it's head down; get the play under my belt. Then I'll get over to the Globe and have a look."

He couldn't say why. He knew he could do this role.

Learning the long speeches gradually made sense. Jamie, at nineteen, had never experienced tragedy. Yet, with the death of Sir Donald, a man he had grown to love, he had some insight into many of the lines in the play, such as: *"Why, such is love's transgression. Griefs of mine own lie heavy in my breast."* He had read somewhere that to feel and play a role you needed to experience tragedy, loss or great emotion. He had now been touched by loss. It had gone deep.

In a few weeks, he would be twenty. A milestone. No longer a teenager.

He and Phyllis met up every so often, and she had a problem – not a huge one, but one she was aware could become one. She was strongly attracted to him.

On tour she had noticed him, seen him become a professional, watched his growth, and now here she was, about to embark on one of literature's most passionate relationships with him; she had to be careful.

"Play it cool. Keep the passion for the stage," she convinced herself.

Alix kept in touch.

"A great honeymoon, Jamie: long walks in the glens, swimming in the lochs. You should try it, laddie. It's a great thing, with your woman beside you."

"Maybe I will, Alix. Sounds as though you've been enjoying yourself."

"I tell you, it's been something. There were some great pubs where we stayed. Took part in cèilidhs, and Morag's turned out to be a fair dancer."

"How is Jeannie? Any news?"

"Not so far. Morag will pop in to see her."

"I've got some news, by the way."

"What's that, laddie?"

"Remember my telling you about a Sir Donald Carstairs?"

"I do, indeed. He came to all your performances."

"Well, he has died suddenly."

"Ah, Jamie, that's a sad thing."

"He's left me his estate, in a trust until I'm thirty."

"Good god, Jamie!"

"Thought I should tell you, but keep it to yourself; better that way."

"Mum's the word. I'm pleased for you."

After the agreed month, Jamie and Phyllis met up to practise together. She'd mastered the role well; she had positive ideas on interpretation.

"Are these teenagers just difficult adolescents, because their families forbid their relationship? Do we relate these two children to modern ideas? Today they'd be called 'disturbed'."

"We've got to decide that, I guess."

"Hey, let's not get entangled in modern, complex psychological overtones; let's play it straight, pretend we're in the century it's set in, let it evolve. See what the producer thinks, as well; he has the last word, anyway."

Soon they began to enjoy the exchange of dialogue, mostly working on memory. "When we have it up and running, memory-wise, then let's see where it takes us."

The theatre rang one morning.

"Hi, Jamie. Can you both come for a rough run-through next week?"

"Sure."

"How about Tuesday at ten-thirty a.m.?"

He rang Phyllis.

"That's fine, Jamie. I'll be there."

For the next two months, they became immersed in daily rehearsals and costume fittings. Gradually, the drama was given a shape. The fight scenes, after a tricky start, began to work. The first night drew gradually nearer.

Will I be ready? Jamie asked himself, ever the self-doubter.

"Don't think that, Jamie," Phyllis said, when he happened to mention it over a meal.

"I know."

"I feel exactly the same. It's perfectly normal."

"I'll try."

With two days to go, Alix rang him.

"Jamie, bad news. Morag had a call from the hospital: Jeannie's been gang-raped and badly beaten up. They think she may not survive. Thing is, she wants to see you."

"Oh, God! I've got my first night in two days, Alix."

"I do know that. But I think, if you can, you should come up."

Jamie sought the producer.

"John, I have to go up to Scotland for a night. A person I know has asked for me, and I believe she may be dying. Would that be alright?"

"I guess so. It's a bit near the opening but, as long as something awful doesn't happen, I see no problem. Won't stop me being relieved when you get back, though."

"I promise to phone regularly."

"Okay, Jamie. Before you go, let me just say that I think what you are doing is working."

"Gee, thanks, John. Need lots of that."

The next day, he got a flight to Dundee, the nearest airport to Montrose. Jamie was there to meet him.

"It's not a pretty story, Jamie. Just when Jeannie seemed to be putting it together, this happened. She's dying, and anxious to see you."

"This is awful, Alix. What actually happened?"

"Nobody knows. All I heard is that a fight broke out, and somehow Jeannie became involved. She's badly hurt."

At the Montrose hospital, Jamie went into the ward.

"Let me speak with her alone, Alix."

He searched for Jeannie, not knowing what to expect.

She was in the last bed on his right. A still, sad, little figure, eyes shut, her face bruised; a broken, battered wreck. He sat down beside her.

"Hi, Jeannie. It's me, Jamie."

She didn't seem to hear him.

"Jeannie, can you hear me? It's Jamie."

One good eye opened; the other was shut and black.

"Och, Jamie, that's kind; I wanted to see you… to thank you – the only person to help me, after all I did to you. I just want you to know that."

"You'll get better, Jeannie."

"No, I don't think so; I was sorely beaten. There were five of them."

"Oh, Jeannie, fight it. You have so much to live for."

"I've nothing to live for, Jamie."

"I'll be here for you."

A bruised hand clung to his. "I don't deserve you. But I needed you to know that I will never, ever forget you, Jamie."

"What about your parents?"

"I've never seen them since the day Ma told me to get out."

"I'm sorry, Jeannie. I wish I could have done more."

The effort of speaking seemed to exhaust her. She turned her face and seemed to sleep.

"How was she, Jamie?

"Asleep. I'm glad I came, Alix; I think she needed to tell me how she felt. But, God, Alix, how could this have happened to her?"

"Morag just rang me to explain; I understand she went to a dance in Montrose and it turned into a drunken brawl. They turned on her. What they did was terrible."

"Have you caught anyone?"

"There were five of them. So far, we've arrested three of them."

As they were speaking, a woman came into the waiting room.

"Are you Jamie?"

"Yes."

"I'm Jeannie's mother."

"Well, Jeannie is dying. You're a bit late."

"I know. I've come to see her; to tell her that I'm sorry."

Where was the large, loud-voiced woman, red in the face with anger? Here now was a shrunken, sad person, guilt and remorse written on her wasted face.

"Go in and tell her... something. Anything. That you love her."

She turned without a glance and went in.

The two men left the hospital.

"Better take me to the airport, Alix. Do you mind?"

"Of course not, laddie. I am glad you came, though."

"Yeah, me too. Funny how Jeannie has been in the story for so long, isn't it?"

"I know what you mean. In any other scenario she'd have been a lovely girl, married someone, had a family. What went wrong? I guess we'll never know."

"Funny you put it like that. Doing this play has opened my eyes to families, and how they affect each other. You could put Jeannie into a drama that Shakespeare would have enjoyed."

Alix said goodbye at the airport. "Go back, dear friend. Wow those critics."

"I'll try, Alix."

CHAPTER TWENTY-SEVEN

Jamie phoned the producer as soon as he got back.

"That's a relief," John laughed; "I had imagined all sorts of terrible happenings, and that you wouldn't get back in time."

"Sorry to put you through that."

"Tomorrow, we start the dress rehearsal at ten-thirty a.m."

"I'll be there, John... raring to go."

Later, Phyllis rang him. "I hear you were gallivanting off somewhere. Glad you are back."

"Just something that had to be done. How about meeting up, have a meal, talk things over?"

"That would be nice, Jamie. Let's go back to where we ate the first time."

Putting the phone down, Phyllis was glad to hear Jamie's voice. In the months they had worked together she had fallen head over heels in love with him. She had tried not to, but with their close contact it was unavoidable. Whether he had, too, she couldn't guess. She couldn't explain these feelings, especially as she had never intended to get emotionally involved. She decided that, once the play was over, she would try to see if Jamie reciprocated her feelings. But now they had a job to do. This play was her chance; what she had worked toward. Jamie, too. And, if they succeeded, they would both be off, in the cut-throat world of acting. They had the chance of their lifetimes.

"Concentrate, Phyllis," she exhorted herself. "Don't blow it because of a beautiful face."

At the restaurant that evening, all they could talk about was tomorrow's final rehearsal.

"How do you feel we are coming across?" Jamie asked Phyllis.

"Not sure. John seems pleased. I did think our scenes together went well."

"All I know is that I've been lucky to have you as my Juliet."

"Ditto. You know it's our chance, Jamie? I'm scared and exhilarated, both at once."

Next day, they were on stage, as the dress rehearsal got underway. The drama unfolded and weeks of rehearsal fell into place. Jamie had learned to pace himself, and words flowed from him with ease. He felt it, for the first time.

"Here's to my love! O true apothecary! Thy drugs are quick. Thus with a kiss I die."

As he said the final lines, he felt Jeannie was there with him. He had lost Juliet, but he had lost Jeannie, too.

The love scenes went well. The producer had asked for some realism: real kisses, real embraces… Phyllis's warm, soft lips seemed to tell Jamie something.

The rehearsal was over and everyone seemed pleased. Was the rehearsal too good? Better a bad dress rehearsal and a good performance. Jamie couldn't tell either way; he was drained.

"Well done," John said, in the dressing room. "Now all you need is an audience."

"Thanks, John. Gosh, it's hard work, though."

As Jamie went to go home, he saw a woman sitting in the uncovered seats.

"Hello, Jamie." It was Judy, his mother in the T.V. series.

"Judy? Gosh, were you listening?"

"Sure was. And bravo; what a long way you've come. Now, I'm not going to tempt fate, but you are well on the way to being a great Romeo, Jamie."

"Gosh, thanks for that – especially from you."

"Well, I am telling you, just relax – as if you can, I know, but try to enjoy it. Let me tell you, there will never be a role for you as perfect as this one; you'll remember it all your life, even when you are an old man."

"Thanks, Judy."

"Goodbye, dear boy. Give 'em hell."

Phyllis came out. "Was that who I think it was?"

"It was. She was in the T.V. serial with me. Played my mum."

"How did she think we did?"

"Seemed impressed. Bravo to you, Phyllis. I think we make a good partnership, don't you? When this is over, I want to have a chat about something."

"Why not now?"

"Now's not the time. But I have had some thinking to do – in a way, to do with why I went up to Scotland."

Alix rang before they all sat down to dinner.

"Jamie, I wanted to let you know that Jeannie died this morning. She had no fight left in her. I thought you should know."

"Thanks, Alix. I'm not surprised. Poor Jeannie. What a waste of a life."

"Aye, we did all we could. Now, get on and do a great Romeo, dear friend."

That evening, he had a meal with Michael and Mary.

"We'll all be there," Mary told him. "Mum and Dad are coming down. You will be amazed to know that your aunt and uncle in Montrose are coming down, too. Your uncle, so Ma told me, is grumbling, but I gather he always does."

"Yes, a real moaner, he disapproves of everything. It's amazing that he has agreed."

"Well, your aunt is determined."

"Good for her."

That night, he slept soundly. No dreams. No waking up feeling sick. In his heart, he knew he could do it. Those actors' genes, honed over centuries, were ready. It might not be in the same Globe Theatre stage that Shakespeare had played on, but it would be difficult not to feel his presence.

His mother and father came down in time for the performance, tactfully leaving Jamie alone.

Messages came from the family, and one from Morag and Alix: *"Rooting for you."*

Phyllis was ready, dressed and made up. Hair in plaits made her look so young.

"Toi, toi. Let's give it to 'em."

"Yes, Jamie. Feel good."

He put some good luck cards into all the other dressing rooms.

Trouble was, right now, after waking up so sure, he began to get cold feet. Or "terror" might describe it better! All that early confidence began to drain away. In an hour he would be out there, onto that bare Globe stage; no curtain to hide behind. The London audience. No longer in the backwoods; the anonymous theatre. Would he remember his lines? He couldn't even think of the first one. Oh, God, he would fail! What cheek, to think he could do it.

Sitting in his dressing room, half made up, seeing himself in the mirror, he felt panic.

A knock came at the door.

"Come in."

It was his father.

"Just came to wish you all the best, Jamie."

"Dad, I can't do it!"

"I thought so. Hey, son, it's normal; called 'stage actors' fright'. It will disappear as soon as you walk on. If you didn't have it, I'd worry."

"Honest?"

"Yes, honest. Just do your thing. You know you can do it."

Then it was time.

Walking out, his legs felt a bit wobbly.

He cleared his mind of every thought. He was Romeo. He was walking the streets. He would see Juliet.

He forgot the audience out there. No need to wrack his brains to remember the text; he knew it. How beautiful Juliet was.

Phyllis responded to every mood, every nuance of Shakespeare's words.

He walked through the play. Tomorrow he would remember nothing.

He suffered that Juliet was dead. He couldn't live anymore, drinking the poison and dying. The last words were said. It was over.

Nobody moved. The audience, just for a moment, stayed their claps.

Then thunderous applause broke out. "Bravo!" was shouted.

The cast lined up. Phyllis held Jamie's hand.

"Bravo, love," Jamie whispered.

"You, too," Phyllis replied. "We'll never forget this, will we?"

"That's what Judy said."

He looked down at the audience. There, on the front row, was an empty seat.

Nobody knew – they never would know – that it was for Sir Donald. There he would have sat and revelled in his protégé's success.

It was over. Jamie had not the foggiest idea if he had pulled it off; other people would have to decide.

Backstage he went, to his dressing room.

No time to think; soon his dressing room was full of people. First in were Michael, Mary and Mark.

"Great, Jamie! Brought it all off brilliantly."

"The reviews will be out by morning," Mark told him; "I'll let you have them. Personally, I think they should be good."

Behind them came his B-and-B friends.

"Brill, Jamie!" Willy exclaimed, as they crowded in.

"Oh, you were marvellous," whispered Clarissa.

The biggest surprise was Morag and Alix.

"Couldn't miss it," Alix laughed. "Och, Jamie, that was something."

Behind them stood a crowd of people who, for a minute, Jamie didn't recognize: Gloria, James, Norman and Bob.

"Oh, my god! Great to see you."

"Couldn't miss supporting our two friends," James said.

"All began with you, really," Jamie laughed.

"It was fun, wasn't it?" Gloria agreed. "I knew you'd make it, darling. Can always tell; it's a sort of feeling I get. And I tell you, honey, your Romeo is the sexiest I've seen yet."

Jamie laughed. "Oh, come on, Gloria. I didn't think about him like that."

"Whether you did or not, dear, that's how it came over."

Just as they all left, another couple came in: Aleksi and Olga.

"Jamie, my dear boy, proud of you am I! Everyone at restaurant sends their love and congratulations. Who would have thought just a short time ago you served food in my restaurant?" cried Aleksi.

"You were wonderful, Jamie," whispered Olga.

As people drifted off, and Jamie began to remove his make-up, a knock came at his door. Jamie didn't recognize the man who came in.

"Just to say well done. Your first Romeo, I understand?"

"Yes, it is."

"We haven't met. I'm the director of the Shakespeare Theatre Company. Would you be interested in joining the junior section of the company?"

"Wow, would I?! Sounds interesting. What would it mean?"

"It gives you the opportunity to learn the roles, work alongside seasoned players and generally develop your repertoire. I'm asking Phyllis, as well."

"Can I talk to my agent, and maybe he could get in touch?"

"That would be fine. I know Mark, so I will contact him."

He left after a handshake, leaving Jamie stunned.

Phyllis came in.

"Hey, Jamie, what do you think?"

"My god, Phyllis, I never thought this could happen."

"It feels a bit like getting on a train that won't stop. But I'm not pushing it."

"That's what I feel. So, we stay on board, see where it takes us."

"Know what you mean. Guess we made it tonight, kiddo."

Linda and John came in.

"Mum, Dad, I wondered where you were."

"Thought we'd let the crowd go. Well done, Jamie. Tonight is a long way from that first newspaper-boy debut," John smiled.

Linda was crying. "You had me in tears – in fact, I still am. Proud tears." She sobbed on her son's shoulder.

Soon, everyone had gone. It was over. He'd done it.

Judy was right: he'd never forget his first Romeo.

But now he had something else to do.

Next morning, after a dream-filled sleep, in which he had spent the early hours reciting monologues he had never seen, he woke to the realization that life would never be the same again.

Phyllis rang.

"How are you feeling? I've had an awful night dreaming. In one dream, I was on stage and had forgotten every word of the play. I woke to the sounds of people booing."

"More or less the same for me. Maybe this always happens."

"I suppose, after months of concentrating on the play, the mind plays tricks."

"I have no idea. Anyway, let's meet for lunch. Same restaurant at twelve-thirty?"

"Okay, see you there."

He arrived before she did and ordered a drink.

He was nervous.

For Jamie had decided something. He had fallen in love with Phyllis.

In those love scenes, when Romeo and Juliet had spent a night together, urged on by the producer – "Make it look real, guys" – on a stage watched by people and tonight by several hundred, she had, in giving those warm, sweet kisses, her body lying so close, stirred his natural emotions.

The fears that the Jeannie trauma had evoked, he now knew, had finally gone. His visit to Scotland, seeing Jeannie again, knowing a life had been spoiled, had made him determined to make sure that his love was what he wanted. He'd always been afraid that he was a prig. *"I only wanted to do what Jeannie offered with the woman I loved and would marry."* Had that sounded priggish from a sixteen-year-old boy? Probably did, but he had meant it. And he felt now that he had found that woman.

Phyllis came in.

"Hi, Jamie. Great to meet up here again; I'll always have a soft spot for it. It was here we planned our future, and now we can celebrate."

"Let's order, then let's talk."

What does he want? Phyllis asked herself. Jamie looked excited. He had a way of whistling gently through his teeth when he had something important to say.

After ordering, he looked at Phyllis.

"This has been coming for some time, Phyllis. Oh, God, how do I say it?"

"Yes, Jamie?"

"Wanted to say this for some time."

"Are you proposing, Jamie?" she asked.

"I reckon I am. Never done it before. But yes. I love you."

"Then I accept. For I've loved you for a long time."

"You have? Why didn't you tell me?"

"Oh, come on, Jamie; a girl doesn't do that. We may belong to the twenty-first century, but I'm not the one to make the move."

"Right. So, I ask you: will you be my girl?"

"Yes, Jamie, I will."

"So, now we walk off, hand in hand, into the horizon. That's as satisfactory an ending as I can conjure up."

Printed in Great Britain
by Amazon